"Aw nuts," he said  on the door. He was

And he was startl

could reach it, and

snug green silk dr

threshold. In her right hand she carried a glittering evening purse with a gold chain and a diamond clasp; in her left hand she carried a large, curved knife whose silver hilt was studded with rubies. She smiled and turned sideways, her chest pushing at the silk, her hip doing the same. Then she positioned her spike-heeled black shoes to better balance her weight.

"Jesus," he said, backing away toward the kitchen.

"Hello, Lincoln," she said, and threw the knife at him.

THE
PATCH
OF THE
ODIN
SOLDIER

Look for these Tor books by Geoffrey Marsh

THE KING OF SATAN'S EYES
THE PATCH OF THE ODIN SOLDIER
THE TAIL OF THE ARABIAN, KNIGHT

GEOFFREY MARSH

THE PATCH OF THE ODIN SOLDIER

TOR

A TOM DOHERTY ASSOCIATES BOOK

THE PATCH OF THE ODIN SOLDIER

Copyright © 1987 by Geoffrey Marsh

Reprinted by arrangement with Doubleday & Company, Inc.

First Tor Edition: July 1988

A TOR Book

Published by Tom Doherty Associates, Inc.
49 West 24th Street
New York, NY 10010

ISBN: 0-812-58582-8
Can No.: 0-812-58583-6

Printed in the United States of America

0 9 8 7 6 5 4 3 2 1

To Robert Vardeman:
For showing me that a B.O.H.
Can be a true blossom indeed

ONE

THE MOOSE OF MAINE WERE MISSING. DESPITE THEIR ungainly size, uncommon strength, and continual defiance of the adage that even the ugliest of God's creatures have some beauty in them, they were proving this particular summer to be devilishly elusive, a fact not necessarily bad or unsettling unless one were a hunter intent on breaching the statutes of the Pine Tree State in order to rack up a trophy for a den or a law office.

The area around Great Pass Lake was typical of the countryside in all respects including the missing moose—the mountains were high and darkly forested, the lakes clear and perfect reflectors of the sky, which held the occasional billowing cloud sweeping over from the Canadian border, the air sharp with the scent of pine and flower, and the human population as limited as Nature could make it on short notice. The roads, when there were any and they hadn't been laid down by now defunct logging companies, were barely two lanes and tended to hug the contours of the land tighter than a gigolo hugs his matron. But they were serviceable, and as long as it didn't snow they sped the local to work or to home, and the tourist comfortably on his way to his destination—preferably to New Hampshire or Massachusetts.

Great Pass itself was an impressive notch in the Longfellow Mountains; it was the apex of an inverted triangle whose western point was Moosehead Lake and whose northeastern tip was the town of Millinocket. The Pass itself was reached by a dirt road picked up ten miles out of Brownville Junction, at the four-corner hamlet of Paccatornet, and the lake was just beyond, in a pocket valley two miles on a side and hidden from most by the nature of its accessibility. It was not a large lake, nor even a particularly spectacular one as Maine lakes go, but it was the centerpiece of a meadow lined by massive pines that cast shadows long before dark, and it was fed by a large stream at its eastern end, emptying into a larger one at the west when the beaver weren't busy and the rains were on schedule.

So far off the beaten trail was it that the only ones to visit its shores in the month of August had been a party of lost hunters still looking for moose.

And Lincoln Bartholomew Blackthorne.

The cabin was constructed on the eastern shore, just ahead of the rocky slope of Great Pass Mountain, and just below the Great Pass itself. It was made of seasoned, still-barked logs closely joined and sealed with mud from the lake's bed; there were two large windows in front, one on either side, and two in back. A porch with a slightly sagging roof faced the water two hundred yards distant, and the shingled roof was broken only by the sturdy top of the fireplace chimney. The land ahead of the cabin had been cleared a while ago, though no attempt had been made to turn the wild grasses and flowers into a lawn. Trees overhung it, there was a shed on its left, and just to its right was a large-mouthed well with an old oaken bucket resting on the lip.

It was warm this third week of August, and dragonflies hovered listlessly over the reeds, bees limped from blossom to blossom, and back in the woods one could hear the limpid scolding of several birds disturbed by a bear heading for Quebec.

Lincoln sat in a rocking chair on the porch and smiled, his face partially covered by the sagging brim of a fly-festooned fishing hat, his booted feet propped up on the rough-hewn railing. He enjoyed listening to the orchestral arrangements of the forest around him, the lake slapping the shore at twilight, the stream to his right splashing over the rocks; he hummed along with the birds, chuckled at the groans of bears sorting out their territory, and waited patiently for the indelicate bellow of a moose hunting its mate.

That was the only disappointment this year—there were no moose, at least not at Great Pass.

Had he been a less content person, he would have turned right around and returned to his tailor shop in Inverness, New Jersey; he would have swallowed his pride and allowed to his friends that all his complaints about never having seen a moose in the wild were not satisfied, despite the fact that doing just such a thing was the avowed purpose of the trip.

But he knew that sooner or later life would provide him with a moose in its own good time. If it was meant to be, then it was meant to be; and if it wasn't, there would always be a next time, assuming he didn't get himself killed.

He sighed loudly and stretched his arms over his head.

This was indeed the life.

His vacation had originally been scheduled for just three weeks, and had been postponed because of a side trip to New Mexico he was trying to forget; but once begun it had left three weeks behind and stretched, thus far, into five. A few hasty letters from his friends in Inverness wanted to know if he had abandoned the shop for emulation of Natty Bumppo, and he had sent only a postcard in reply, assuring one and all that he was merely making up for lost time—it was, when all was said and done, the first true vacation he had had in nearly a decade, and he wasn't about to cut it short just because his business needed him.

It was a truth, despicable or otherwise, that he did not need it.

There were plenty of tailors in Sussex County who could suit his customers if emergencies had been declared; and plenty of shops in nearby malls where slick smiling salesmen could con the green from a man faster than the man could step back from the cold-handed measurement of his one and only inseam.

He, on the other hand, did not exactly have money to burn, but certainly enough to insure a comfortable old age should he be fortunate enough to reach such an earthly plateau. It was true he had enemies, and it was true they were constantly attempting to plug him into the insurance companies' fine-tuned statistics, and it was also true that he got himself easily into more trouble than the average tailor on an average day in an average but uneventful year.

Yet, he thought, it was a burden he was usually willing to shoulder once he returned to civilization —as long as he could spot his goddamned moose.

He sighed again and watched as the sun was speared by the ridge across the lake. The water had turned dark, the sky to indigo laced through with rose, and a lone cloud scudded north to south. A flock of mallards soared over the cabin and landed with admirable precision along the western shoreline. Their calls made him smile, and he listened so intently he did not hear the footsteps rounding the corner.

When he did, instead of leaping to his feet and snapping out the knife he habitually kept in a sheath on his left wrist, he turned his head indolently and stared at the figure approaching the steps.

"Don't bother," he said when a hiking boot lifted to climb the first stair. "I'm not in the market."

"Now, Mr. Blackthorne," said Owen Kintab, "it ain't right you should be here all this time without tryin some."

Lincoln shook his head. "I'm not interested."

"Cheaper than the stores."

"No," he said, and deliberately looked away from the lanky man in the red plaid hunting jacket, rounded red cap, and dark red trousers tucked into red boots. He was young, in his mid-twenties, and didn't seem strong enough to lift a pebble much less hike with a forty-pound pack through the high notch from Great Pass Village. At least once a week, however, Kintab did just that, trying to sell his illegal venison and bear steaks, solemnly declaring on his mother's as yet undug grave that even the most sophisticated Down East gourmet over to Bangor seldom had an opportunity to tantalize his taste buds with fare like this.

Lincoln demurred easily on the side of legality; besides, eating venison would be like taking a bite out of Bambi, and what would Thumper do for fun then? Bear steaks he refused to even contemplate, considering the odor that wafted from the pack whenever Owen brought them along.

Kintab pushed his cap to the back of his head, gave the tailor a look of mercantile disgust, and unshouldered his oversized red backpack. "Brought your beer, anyways." He yanked on a zipper, pulled out two six-packs and left them on the top step. "Ain't very cold. You want me t' put em in the water?"

"No, thanks, I can do it." He reached into his jeans pocket and pulled out a bill, glanced at it, and tossed it in the air. Kintab moved swiftly, his left hand out and in his own pocket before Lincoln could blink.

"Much obliged."

"Anytime."

"Sure you don't want—"

"I'm sure."

"You city boys don't know what you're missin."

"I'll pass."

Kintab shrugged, replaced the pack, and started off. At the corner of the porch, however, he snapped his fingers, stopped, and looked over his shoulder. "Some people at the store lookin for you, Mr. Blackthorne."

Lincoln slowly lowered his feet to the floor. "Who?"

"City folks." The young man smiled toothlessly. "Thought they could bribe me, they did. Flashin more money than I've ever seen in m'life. Sure were anxious to find ya."

Lincoln looked the question.

"Nope."

"How many?"

"Two."

"Men?"

"Woman, man, damnedest things I ever did see."

He rose and sat on the railing, scanning the water, suddenly feeling the chill as the sun dipped below the ridge. "What did they say?"

Kintab turned around, deftly caught another bill before the night breeze took it, and shrugged the pack into a more comfortable position. Then he sniffed, adjusted his cap, and buttoned his jacket. It would be well past midnight before all that red would be invisible to the naked eye.

"The man says he's lookin for you, says he's an old friend of the family and was just passin through." The man chuckled. "The only things what pass through here are the moose, ain't that right, Mr. Blackthorne?"

"What moose," he grumbled.

"What moose? Why, Mr. Blackthorne, one big old bull got into my Aunt May's clothesline just yesterday mornin. Tore her sheets to ribbons, it did. Took me and May four hours to chase the critter away."

"That," Lincoln said with a scowl, "is unkind, Owen. What else did he say?"

"Nothin much. Just flashed that money around and asked me again."

"Did you take it?"

"Yep. You think I'm a fool?"

"Where did you send him?"

"Over to Bangor. Told him you was sick and tired of the mosquitoes eatin you alive and was gonna rent my rich cousin's air-conditioned house, the one with the ugly bats on the fence to keep the bugs away. Said you said you wasn't comin back until next year."

Lincoln nodded. "Who was the woman?"

"Wife, I suppose."

He nodded again. And doubted it. "Take off, Owen. I got to get some sleep."

"Sure thing, Mr. Blackthorne," Kintab said, tipping his hat and backing into the shadows. "Sure thing. You take care, hear? We don't want you all tuckered out, now do we?"

Lincoln did not reply, but waited until he could no longer hear the man pushing along the trail toward the Pass. Once he was positive he was alone, he went into the cabin and switched on the lamp nearest the door.

The front room was thirty feet on a side, the left portion the living area complete with a fieldstone fireplace large enough to put a couch in, the right the dining room with a small table, four chairs, and the walls covered with glass-fronted bookcases. The floors were covered by a series of thick, hand-braided rugs, the ceiling was low with its beams exposed, and in the center of the rear wall was a china closet skillfully refitted to hold a meager selection of firearms and knives. To the left of the closet was the door to his bedroom, to the right the open door to the kitchen. The room was cold, and he wasted no time laying a fire, then kneeling before it to consider his options.

In the first place, he doubted that Owen's story had gotten rid of the couple. Whoever had been to Paccatornet had known just where to find him, and they were only checking to see if he was known to the natives. Owen, always on the look for an increase in his pension, probably told the truth, but just as probably wasn't believed.

In that case, sometime in the next twenty-four hours he was going to have company. The question was, did he put on the kettle or take out the rifle?

"Well, damn," he muttered as he pushed himself to his feet. It always happened, just when he was getting to like the quiet. While he could not complain this time that he didn't have his vacation at last, he could certainly protest the way it was interrupted.

On the other hand, the visitation, whatever it meant and whenever it would be, might just be a friendly visit from an old pal or two.

On the other hand save that one, the only friends he had in Maine were Owen Kintab and his kin, and the only friends who knew where he was were sweltering down in New Jersey. Which meant that either some of his Inverness friends were trying to reach him when they knew he didn't want to be reached; or his customers were more anxious than he had thought for their fall ensembles; or he was being stalked.

He tossed a mental coin, and went straight to the gun case, opened it, and pulled out a .44 Magnum. From a drawer in the base he extracted a clip, loaded it, and stuffed two more into his shirt pockets. Then he went into the kitchen and turned on the stove, slipped a frozen Italian dinner into the oven, and returned to the living room to wait.

One way or another, one of his appetites would be satisfied.

"Aw nuts," he said then, when someone knocked on the door. He was hoping for the food.

And he was startled when it opened before he could reach it, and a tall redheaded woman in a snug green silk dress stepped lightly over the threshold. In her right hand she carried a glittering evening purse with a gold chain and a diamond clasp; in her left hand she carried a large, curved knife whose silver hilt was studded with rubies. She smiled and turned sideways, her chest pushing at the silk, her hip doing the same. Then she positioned her spike-heeled black shoes to better balance her weight.

"Jesus," he said, backing away toward the kitchen.

"Hello, Lincoln," she said, and threw the knife at him.

TWO

LINCOLN'S REFLEXES HAD NOT YET BEEN FATALLY dulled by the weeks of somnolence he had fostered in the isolated cabin—his right hand snapped out and neatly grabbed the dagger's hilt as it passed by his ear, and he just managed not to wince at the burning that spread over his palm. Then he looked at the weapon, tossed it in the air, and caught it again while the redhead slinked with a pout to the couch and sat down, crossed her legs, and made absolutely sure he could see some of the pasture-land gleaming above her knee.

"Okay, where is he?" he asked resignedly, moving to sit in a battered and comfortable armchair facing the couch over a crudely made pine coffee table.

"Here!" a man bellowed with laughter as he plunged through the open door. "Here I am, you old sea dog, you!"

Lincoln only held up the dagger and pointed to the couch, and waited while Arturo Pigmeo whirled to close the door, then bounced across the room and launched himself onto the cushion. He was a short man, barely high enough to reach the center of Lincoln's chest, his curly black hair in a shambles over his forehead and ears; his tuxedo was black, his studs rubies, and the coat he wore around his shoulders the finest, though dated, vicuña.

"Lincoln, my dear old friend!"

Pigmeo never spoke; he exclaimed, he exhorted, he wailed and, whenever he thought it proper, he sang.

"Art."

Pigmeo squirmed deliciously into the corner and grinned at the redhead, grinned at Lincoln and, after a palms-up gesture to prove he wasn't going for a weapon, he reached into his jacket. A fanfare and flourish, and he tossed a large manila envelope onto the table. There was no name or address written on it, no stamps, and it was thick as a man's hand. Lincoln stared at it as though expecting it to speak, then raised an eyebrow in a shrug and made an elaborate show of examining the dagger. The hilt's jewels, he noted with a certain premonitory dismay, were artfully arranged around a delicate etching of a figure wearing a horned helmet, with one hand raised to brandish a sword over its head. Turning the weapon over, he saw a similar figure on the other side, outlined in emeralds.

On the blade itself was a swirl of runes.

Arturo stretched his arm over the back of the couch, crossed his legs at the knee, and nodded. "You see, my friend, how exquisite is that weapon. How magnificent is the style, how perfect the balance. A man would give his soul to own a treasure like that, don't you think?"

"It's pretty," he said cautiously.

"Pretty?" Pigmeo's tiny face darkened. "Pretty?

Lincoln, my friend of so long ago who saved our lives and quite possibly our fortunes, do you have any idea how old that artifact is? Have you any idea of the invaluable intrinsic wealth and historical worth attached to that superbly forged weapon of destruction?"

"No."

Pigmeo nodded as if his point had been decisively made, then reached into his jacket's other pocket and pulled out yet another large manila envelope. Linc was beginning to suspect he carried them around to make his chest look bigger.

"Now, then," Pigmeo said with a clap of his hands, "to business."

"Now, then," Lincoln said quietly, "how did you find me?"

Pigmeo's self-assured smile faltered at the tailor's tone, and he looked quickly to his companion, who was busy smoothing the shimmering silk down over her chest and lap, clucking when the wrinkles would not vanish at her command. When she did not respond to his silent plea, he sniffed and ignited a cigarette with a silver lighter, blew the smoke loudly toward the ceiling, and sucked at his cheeks.

"We asked around," the woman said then, her voice as deep as a man's.

"Asked around where?"

After several deliberate seconds, she deigned to grant him a gaze with eyes as green as her evening dress, and he met it with one just as steady, and just as impersonal. A shrug, a moue of annoyance, and she accepted a cigarette from Pigmeo without bothering to check if it were lit.

"Well?"

"We were on vacation," she said, staring at the wall behind him. "We like to drive around and see how normal people live. Arturo says that normal people live in small towns. We took out a map and found a small town. We drove there. We looked around. We realized it was your small town, so we asked about you. They told us you were here. We drove here because we have not seen you in a very long time."

"Salome," he said sincerely, "you are a stunning woman."

Her nod was acceptance of the compliment and a request that he tell her something she didn't already know. But he said nothing more, remembering instead the last time he had met this pair, and the trouble he had gotten into trying to keep Pigmeo from being incarcerated by some bothersome law enforcement officials in Augusta, Georgia. They had tried to rob a museum, and he had been there at the time, attempting to purchase a Cree artifact for a client of his. The museum wouldn't sell, and as he had turned to leave, Pigmeo and Salome Testa had strolled in with machine guns at the ready, and half the police force right behind them. It had taken him several hours and a dozen telephone calls to prove that he was not only a tailor, but a procurer of items valuable or not, for people willing to pay his expenses. He claimed, not precisely accurately, that the demonstrative pair were part of his team—mere apprentices with a flair for the dramatic—and he would be more than glad to fire them on the spot. Which he did, after extracting a promise from

Pigmeo that they never, on the pain of his becoming even shorter than he was, see each other again.

"You are also trying to sell me the Brooklyn Bridge."

She looked at him, puzzled. *"Cómo?"* she asked.

"Perry," he said. "C'mon, give."

He waited for another explanation, cleaning his nails with the blade and eventually losing patience and staring pointedly at Pigmeo's midsection.

Arturo got the message.

Salome fluffed her hair and flicked ashes on the carpet.

Outside the cabin, an owl called, and something larger and less friendly answered.

Arturo looked nervously over his shoulder at the dark window, then squirmed to the edge of his cushion and picked up the second envelope. He opened it and spilled seven photographs onto the surface. Carefully, humming a medley of Teutonic arias under his breath, he arranged them so that Lincoln could see without straining. Then he patted Salome's knee confidently and cleared his throat.

"My friend," he said, "we have made this arduous trek into your country's most luscious and verdant wilderness because we should like to avail ourselves of your expert services in the field of the retrieval of certain items not ordinarily found among the possessions of the general population. Wonderful, eh?"

"On a cold day in hell, Art," he said, and dropped the dagger on top of the pictures.

"Now, now, my friend, let's not be hasty."

"Hasty makes pudding, old pal, and I am on vacation, in case you hadn't noticed. If you want me to take care of that execrable suit so that it fits you properly, I will. If you want me to fix Salome's dress so she can breathe without wheezing, I will. But I am not in the market, as it were, for partners in your class."

Pigmeo gave Salome a pleading look, but she ignored him, concentrating instead on fumbling through her purse. A minute passed, and he shrugged and leaned back, sighing loudly and shaking his head dolefully, then jumped to his feet with a squeal when one of the burning logs snapped in half, sending a curtain of sparks into the flue. He grinned sheepishly, and Lincoln chastised himself for not noting how apprehensive the man was, and how Salome was without her usual flair for seduction. They were a smarmy pair, to be sure, but unlike others he had known, relatively honest.

While Pigmeo paced the hearth then and stared at the fire, Lincoln closed his eyes for a moment, told himself he was asking for trouble if he showed even the slightest mote of interest, but it really was an intriguing dagger and what would it hurt just to look at a few pictures. So he leaned over and picked up the blade, and saw beneath it a color photograph of Salome somewhat without the usual complement of clothing, standing in front of a white wall and holding a horned helmet. In the second she was wearing a fur cloak that had gone out of style when Eric the Red retired; in the third, she was clinging to a detached and fierce dragon masthead whose paint and dyes had long since been chipped and weathered to dullness; in the fourth she held a hide-

and-iron shield almost as large as she was; in the fifth and sixth a suggestive but impressive brace of spears.

Pigmeo took the moment to begin singing, a mournful collaboration between Verdi and Puccini, and one loud enough to bring back the glaciers that had formed the valley.

Lincoln, after restarting his heart, ignored him and looked back at the table.

The seventh photo was a disappointment. It was in black-and-white, and Salome was not included; all he could see was a portion of flooring or a plain table on which stood a figurine either of wood or horn, carved in the same position as the man on the dagger's hilt. In the upper lefthand corner was an inset of the warrior's face—the coarse and cruel visage of a man used to being obeyed without question, and most likely eager to carry out harsh punishment to those who defied him.

The man was wearing a patch.

"Art," he said, with one finger on the warrior's chest, "are you studying the Vikings or something?"

Pigmeo paused in his semi-melodic appeal to the gods only long enough to shake his head before resuming his pacing, switching now to Wagner out of Arthur Sullivan. When Lincoln looked to Salome, she only turned away and pulled a compact from her purse to examine the arch of her eyebrows and the line of soft crimson lipstick around her mouth. It didn't take him long to notice that her hand was trembling.

"All right," he said, leaning back and forcing Pigmeo to stop with a look, "what's going on?"

"On?" Pigmeo repeated, highly insulted. "On, you say? My dear old friend, we are merely interested in obtaining a small item for our modest private collection which will, in the long run and through careful investment, properly provide for our eventual and lamentable retirement! On? My lord, Lincoln, you old sea dog you, whatever—"

"Can it, Art."

Pigmeo strode angrily to the chair, slammed his hands on his hips, and looked him straight in the eye. "It is easy for you to say, my friend."

"I assume," he said blandly, "that since the lovely Miss Testa is in six of those pictures—and rather remarkably, I might add—that it is the statuette you want."

Salome managed a sneer as she reapplied her lipstick.

Pigmeo clasped his hands and looked to the ceiling. "Mona Lisa, such perception! Such analysis! My god, Lincoln, you must make a hell of a summer wardrobe!"

"Art," he warned.

"Yes, I know. I effuse."

Lincoln nodded, and smiled his encouragement.

"And you are right, my friend. Miss Testa and I are seeking that very statue which, figuratively speaking, you have put your finger on."

"Why?"

Pigmeo took a step back and adjusted his coat more snugly on his shoulders. "I have already explained that."

"And where is it?"

Pigmeo never got the opportunity to answer.

Suddenly, there was an enormous commotion outside, as if a vagrant herd of ill-tempered bison had decided to stop roaming and make their home on the cabin porch. The deep thunder of hooves was enough to shake the walls, stir the fire, and make the glasses in the kitchen ring alarmingly. Linc was on his feet instantly, snapping off the lights and heading for the gun case, while Pigmeo and Testa retreated hastily into the bedroom.

The racket continued unabated, and something began pounding on the door. Salome shrieked hysterically and ran from the bedroom into the kitchen; Pigmeo poked his head around the jamb and asked timidly if Linc needed help before running from the bedroom to the hearth where he picked up a poker.

Linc, meanwhile, had eschewed the Magnum as a bit of overkill and had taken down a shotgun from its rack; he loaded it, and moved quickly around the chair to the window where, pulling aside the curtain, he tried to see what was attacking his home away from home.

The pounding continued, and it wasn't long before the thick iron hinges began to bend.

A plate shattered in the kitchen, and Salome ran with a sob back into the bedroom and slammed the door; Pigmeo dropped the poker when the top hinge snapped and the door began to splinter, and ran into the kitchen; Linc could see nothing but a huge dark form steadily and singlemindedly butting the door with a rack of antlers too large to have squeezed through had he opened it on the first request.

Damn, he thought, I've found my first moose.

Salome ran out of the bedroom, snatched up her purse, and ran back, reslamming the door and relocking it without apology; Pigmeo stood in the kitchen doorway with an iron skillet in his hand, trembling but refusing to leave his dear old friend to the mercy of the beast that now snapped the bottom hinge and crashed the door into the room.

Lincoln backed to the far wall and aimed the shotgun.

The noise stopped.

All he could hear was Salome whimpering, Pigmeo puffing, and a soft but angry snorting out on the porch.

The fire snapped, and another log cracked.

"Lincoln," Arturo whispered, sidling fearfully to stand beside him, "I think we may have somehow unwittingly attracted that beast into your living room."

He had thought the same thing, but he suspected it wasn't the pungent perfume Salome was wearing.

"Perhaps," the small man continued with a wary eye on the moose, "I should attempt to distract the creature while you fill it full of lead."

It was a tempting idea, and he was trying to remember where you shot a rampaging moose to keep it from rampaging through your house when the moose decided it was tired of waiting. It charged the doorway again, splintering the frame and wedging its massive head and antlers into the room. Before Lincoln could squeeze off the first round, Arturo shrieked, threw the skillet at the beast's nose and ran for the bedroom. In the course of his panicked flight, he knocked the shotgun from Linc's hands, slammed through the bedroom door and locked it behind him.

Linc stood then in the middle of the room, while the bull moose took his measure, and lowered its head for the charge.

THREE

"TAKE IT EASY," LINC SAID AS HE SIDLED TOWARD THE shotgun. "Just take it easy, fella."

"Sure thing," the moose said, and obligingly dropped its head on the floor.

It took a second or two before the voice sank in. Then he swore softly and switched on the lamps, staring as Owen shrugged out of his portion of the mangy animal costume, reached behind him, and yanked on a zipper. It took him several attempts to get it moving in the right direction, and when he finally managed it there was a relieved groan from outside, then a giggle as Aunt May Kintab walked in with the moose's hindquarters draped over her shoulder. She winked broadly at him, and dropped the disguise onto the floor.

"What the hell are you doing here?" he asked, not sure if he should be furious or grateful.

"Suit needed airin," Owen said, kicking it aside.

"Smells like moose," his aunt declared.

"You ever smell a moose?" the young man asked. Lincoln shook his head.

"Like bear gone bad, this time of year." He wrinkled his nose for effect, then hitched at his baggy jeans.

"I repeat," Lincoln said, unable to sound as stern as he wanted, "what the hell are you two doing here?"

"Cavalry," May told him, brushing her vivid white hair away from a forehead creased less with age than with a life not found in Portland society. She smiled. "To the rescue."

Lincoln gaped, then remembered his panicked visitors, and with a silent order for the Kintabs to remain where they were, he hurried into the bedroom. With only the glow from the living room, there were only shadows and shapes, but he knew immediately it was empty. A cautious step in, and a sudden chilly breeze made him look to the back wall—the window was broken, all the glass smashed from its frame. He checked the closet just to be sure Art hadn't changed his mind, then leaned on the sill, and thought he heard the sound of rapid movement deep in the woods. A sigh, and he returned to the front, dropped into his chair and waited until the Kintabs, aunt and nephew, had taken places on the couch.

"And what," he said then, "made you two think I needed rescuing?"

May, who was twice the age and twice the width of Owen, plucked at her shirt and blew a strand of hair from her eyes. "Saw that tart with a gun."

"Gun?"

"Gun. Little bitty one."

"Where?"

"In her purse. Saw it through the window. Owen here, he didn't much like them two."

"Nope," Owen said with a sharp nod. "Somethin fishy about em, if you know what I mean. Can't trust a man what sings in a foreign language all the time."

"Didn't look right," May added. "Weren't exactly wearin the right kind of clothes for the country, if you see what I see. She have that thing painted on or somethin?"

Owen chuckled, and laughed aloud when his aunt slugged him none too gently on the arm.

Linc supposed he should be grateful. He was ashamed to admit he hadn't seen the weapon Salome had had, and would not have been surprised if, on his continuing refusal to work for them, she had decided to add another element to her persuasive abilities. He was disappointed; he had rather hoped she would have gone the usual route.

"Besides," Owen said, "don't like folks who don't believe me when I lie to them."

May patted his arm sympathetically. "Not to worry, nephew," she said. "Expect they ain't gonna stop ambulating until they reach Georgia."

"How do you know about Georgia?" Linc demanded.

"I went to school, ninny. I ain't pretty, but I ain't dumb either."

He managed to look properly abashed, then picked up the thick envelope still lying on the coffee table and turned it over slowly in both hands. The

24

second one was missing, and he supposed that Arturo, despite his panicked flight, had had the presence of mind to snatch it up before he left. He glanced toward the bedroom, won two out of three with a more than willing conscience, and sighed at the burdens life continually forced upon him. Then, as the Kintabs watched, he hefted it, then opened the clasp and flap and looked inside.

"Well, I'll be damned."

There were several packets of money inside, and if the bills beneath were the same denominations as those on top, it amounted to several thousand dollars more than he had in his wallet at the moment. It made him think. It made him wonder if Pigmeo and Testa weren't actually legitimate this time.

"Aunt May," Owen said with some embarrassment when he saw the look on Lincoln's face, "I think we didn't exactly do right here, this time."

"Oh dear," she said sorrowfully, and gripped her hands in her lap. "Oh dear, Mr. Blackthorne, I hope you aren't . . . that is, we didn't trust them folks none, if you can understand that from the look of them. And Owen allowed as how we oughta take a look-see, find out if you was in trouble."

"Moose was just hangin around," the nephew said. "Figured it was as good as any for chasin off city folk."

"All right," he said, waving them silent. "I understand, and I'm thankful for the concern. You weren't to know they were, for them, on the up-and-up this time."

Aunt May, however, still seemed depressed, and

Owen put a consoling arm around her shoulder. They sat there for several seconds before May suddenly slapped her hands on her thighs and stood.

"Well, that's that, I always say. Come, Owen, we'll leave the man to his thoughts."

Owen rose and followed her to the door, picking up the costume along the way. "If we find em, Mr. Blackthorne, should we send em back to ya?"

"If you find them," he said absently.

"Sorry again," May said from the door. "But you come on back to my place before you go, I'll fix you a whoppin meal, one of my specialties."

He looked up and smiled, unable to find anything more than faint annoyance in his heart. "I'll do that."

"Mr. Blackthorne," Owen said then.

"What?"

"Think you might want to walk outside with us?"

He shook his head. "Don't think so."

"Think you better."

"Why's that?"

"Think the cabin's gonna blow up."

Lincoln started to laugh, and caught himself when he saw May leap over the threshold and vanish into the night.

"Gotta nose," Owen said, tapping the appendage with a forefinger. "Can smell a fuse a mile away. This one ain't no mile away, though. Think it's behind the cabin. You gonna come, or what?"

Lincoln jammed the packets of money into his shirt, grabbed up the shotgun and his windbreaker, and was hard on Owen's racing heels, halfway to

26

the lake, when he saw Aunt May drop to the ground. He didn't ask questions; he dropped.

And the cabin blew up.

Squinting against the brief, red, daylight glare and the rush of hot air that rippled his clothes and seemed to scorch his hair, he saw a mushroom cloud of fire lift from the clearing toward the stars, scattering timber in its own wind, scorching the nearest trees, and leveling the well. The sound deafened him. Flaming debris dropped all around them, and twice he had to slap at his legs to smother a bothersome ember. He heard May swearing and Owen exclaiming wonder before the night reclaimed itself and they staggered to their feet.

"Well!" May said, clucking and spitting.

"Gee," said her nephew, brushing dirt from his shirt.

Cautiously, they approached the devastation. A few limbs were still burning, twigs on the ground had turned to momentary tiny torches, but the recent damp weather had prevented the worst of the fire from spreading, and there was little enough left of the cabin to do anything much but smolder.

"Sorry about this," he said, moving as close as he dared to the pit of hot charcoal.

"Not to worry," the young man said. "I can do it again before next year."

May wrung her hands and stared in despair.

"Think it was them? Them in the funny clothes?" Owen asked as they circled the foundation, looking for salvage and clues to the bomb's parents.

"I doubt it," he muttered as he kicked aside a small pile of rubble. "They didn't want to kill me."

"The lady had a gun," he was reminded.

"True, but she wouldn't have shot me. It was to convince me to work with them, that's all. Besides, without her glasses she can't see more than five feet."

"Woman like that wears glasses? No kiddin." Kintab picked up a scrap of twisted metal that used to be a revolver. It was hot. He dropped it and rubbed a palm over his leg. "Thought they had things so you didn't have to."

"She won't wear contacts. She says it destroys the natural gleam in her eye."

Owen sniffed. "Don't rightly know if anyone ever looked at her eyes, Mr. Blackthorne."

"She does," he said. "Constantly."

"City folk," he muttered, and after dropping cooling planks over the opening of the well, they rejoined his aunt, who was holding half a rack of moose antler.

"Your Uncle Edward shot this critter," she said with a catch in her voice. "One shot, right between the eyes. Fell right on him, crushed him to a pancake, we buried him under the roses."

Owen hugged her while she wept, and Lincoln prowled the site again before the tiny fires died and all he was left with was moonlight. But there was nothing to find. The destruction was complete, even to the collapse of the chimney in back.

Fortunately, the damage was not so great to the storage shed, which in spite of the explosion managed to retain a third of its roof and two of its walls.

After a brief consultation and a testing of the wind, he and Owen lugged out four pails which they filled from the nearby stream. Then they proceeded to douse as many of the embers as they could to prevent the wind from taking sparks into the woods. They moved around the immediate vicinity and tossed water on suspect branches, on piles of leaves, on trails of dead needles. They scattered dirt over the cabin's remains, and then they paused and watched as May beat the hell out of a shrub that refused to stop smoking.

When they were finally done and satisfied they could do no more, it was well past midnight, and while the temptation to drop where they were and sleep was great, it was May who suggested that they start for home without delay. Two hours tops, she reminded them, and beds waiting at the other end.

Owen agreed instantly, and Lincoln as well, as soon as he could convince his stinging palms and throbbing legs that he was, in the long run, doing the right thing.

They refused to believe him. Every step of the way up to the Notch and over they screamed, and stabbed at him, and made him stumble over shadows; every step of the way he saw that fiery mushroom cloud, and saw himself spinning inside it, broken and blackened; and every step of the way he wondered who the hell had done it? It definitely wasn't the Kintabs, and he was certain it was neither Testa nor Pigmeo. They had neither the imagination nor the cause to want to see him scattered over ten mountains and a handful of lakes; and they certainly wouldn't have created such an elaborate ruse just to lull him into false security before they blew him up.

It was someone else.

And whether he was the target, or his two visitors, was not as important at the moment as the fact that he was still alive, and that someone else who wanted somebody dead was still out there, unmindful of his failure.

He groaned.

He looked up at the stars and asked silently why, after all this time, he wasn't allowed to have a single moment of solitude without getting into some kind of trouble. He supposed, to be fair in case Someone was listening, that more often than not he managed to bring it on himself. He supposed as well, that given his sideline of hunting down expensive and/or rare objects for various clients who had the desire and the money to see him work, he was bound to run into a spot of difficulty now and then. And he further supposed that his non-superman status lent itself to a mistake once in a while, which in turn led to his slipping unwillingly into varying degrees of danger.

But hell, it was a pain in the ass.

And not for the first time over the past couple of years did he seriously consider giving up the game and settling down at home with his sewing machine, his cloth ruler, and miles of fabric untainted by the synthetic.

In fact, the closer he came to Paccatornet, the more seductive the idea was. All he had to do was find the nearest airport, fly down to Boston, then on to New York, rent a car, and within two hours' leisurely driving, walk into his home and shut his shadow life out behind him.

Then Owen dropped back to walk at his side, arms swinging, lips pulled back over his toothless gums.

"You hangin in there, Mr. Blackthorne?"

Lincoln gasped an affirmative.

May was so far ahead he couldn't see her in the grey light.

"Hope ya don't feel too bad about the cabin."

"It has crossed my mind to help you replace it, yes."

Kintab shook his head. "No need. I need the exercise anyways. Gettin too soft in my old age." And he slapped a hand against the rock of his twenty-six-year-old stomach.

"Amazing," Lincoln said, and wished the damned kid would slow down a bit. It was embarrassing, panting like a dog, sweating like a pig, limping like a horse that had thrown a damned shoe; here he was, a veritable barnyard of decrepitude and disintegration, and Kintab had actually started whistling.

When an owl answered, Kintab shut up.

Fifteen minutes later they left the forest for a narrow dirt lane. May was already gone, and Owen, with a half-smothered chuckle, was prepared to quicken the pace when, with a frown, he slowed and scratched his head.

"Mr. Blackthorne?"

"Yes?"

"You're not thinkin it was them fancy ones that put the dynamite to my cabin, are ya?"

"I thought about it," he said, ignoring his legs, which were slowly buckling at the knees to prove they were serious. "But no, I don't think so. They're not the type."

"My thinkin, too. Couldn't have been them."

"Right."

"Must've been the other one."

Lincoln stopped.

Owen walked ten feet before he realized he was alone.

"Other one?" Lincoln said, praying the explosion had taken out his ears as well as half his muscles.

"Yep."

"I don't want to know."

"Know what?"

"I don't want to know what other one, Owen."

"Oh, that one."

"Which one?"

"The one that come by just before Aunt May and me come up to save you."

FOUR

PACCATORNET QUITE MODESTLY DOES NOT APPEAR ON any but the most meticulous of the area's maps. It is, in fact, so remote and low-key that the Maine legislature hasn't bothered to collect taxes from it in thirty years, reasonably assuming that each time a feisty and reform-ridden member brings it up he's choking. The IRS doesn't have a code for it, and every five or six years the migratory moose plow through it without regard to walls, steps, or precisely-balanced privies. It is, then, in a constant and exciting state of sub-urban renewal.

This summer it consisted, for the most part, of a general store above which lived the elder Kintabs who weren't speaking to each other since the afternoon the old man locked the gas pumps in front so his wife couldn't use them and get all the tips; a modest white house to the right in which Owen continued to live by himself after his wife left with an itinerant Swedish farrier five years before; a stone house on the left that belonged to Aunt May and her deceased husband, subsequently buried in the backyard between the well and the tool shed; and a small cottage to the left of Aunt May's, which was divided into the two efficiency apartments that comprised the entire floor plan of the Paccatornet Motor Lodge. There was also a stable converted into a four-car garage, a bus shelter on the road that ended at the general store, and a telephone booth.

Pigmeo's car, last seen hulked in front of the bus shelter, was gone.

There was no other automobile in sight.

The store's wide porch was lightless, but the moon was high enough for Lincoln to see the black of the surrounding forest. It was enough to make him shiver as he leaned back against the railing and folded his arms across his chest. He wanted nothing more now than to find a soft bed, but he had delayed Owen's departure long enough for May to leave for her own home. Then he and the young man had scouted the area for signs of visitors too shy to announce themselves before they retired to the porch for a cigarette, a sigh, and a contemplation of life's extremities.

Then he had asked again about the other visitor.

"Big fella he was," Owen said, barely visible, his voice adding a decade to his years. "Lean, you understand, but he had to duck just about in half when he come into the store here."

"Basketball player."

"Bigger."

"Damn."

"Had a head of hair out to here, the whitest I ever did see even countin Aunt May. Looked like he combed it with a plow. But he weren't an old coot by a long shot. Face was pretty young. Older'n me, younger'n you."

"Great."

"Ya know him, Mr. Blackthorne?"

"Not yet, I don't think."

"Wore a patch over his left eye."

Lincoln sagged.

"Carried one of them fancified walkin sticks, had a bit ivory handle carved into somethin, I didn't see what."

"Tiger."

Owen frowned and scratched at his chest. "Funny name."

"No. The ivory was carved into a tiger's head. Deep eyes, detail so fine you can probably see the pores if you look close enough. Its mouth is open, and the teeth are so sharp they could cut through a piece of wood."

"He wore a red glove on his left hand."

"Cuts through fingers, too."

Owen shifted, and glanced uneasily at his house. "I wouldn't swear to it, but I think he walked with a limp."

"And shins."

"You know him."

Lincoln nodded with extreme reluctance. "We're acquainted."

"Friend of yours?" Kintab laughed then and flapped his hands. "Never mind. I know a dumb question when I hear one." He held out a hand, a key dangling from a clear plastic room tag. "Don't expect you wanna do much travelin tonight. Room five-seven-three. Bed's all made up."

Lincoln peered at the number embossed on the key. "Owen, there are only two rooms."

"Appearances, Mr. Blackthorne. Makes the tourists feel better, if you see what I see."

He didn't, but neither did he question it. He simply nodded, stepped off the porch and headed for the cottage. His legs were still moaning, his lungs were pumping as fast as his heart, and at the moment he didn't give a damn if the entire Canadian Army charged over the hill in a coup attempt on Bangor—he needed to rest. If he tried to think things out now he'd only confuse himself further.

It was bad enough Arturo and Salome had ferreted out his summer hideaway; now he was marked by someone he hadn't thought he'd see again if he lived to be a thousand.

The last time he had seen Florenz Cull, the man had been dead.

Sleep, when it came, was deep, dreamless, and lengthy. By the time he awakened the next morning, the sun was already high, the air warm, and the tiny room filled with the tempting aroma of bacon and flapjacks. His mouth watering even before he threw aside the covers, Lincoln rubbed his eyes clear and saw a wooden tray sitting on the dresser beside the door. A covered plate, a jug of strong tea, and hot buttered toast. He smiled, fetched the breakfast to the bed, and ate slowly, savoring the meal while wondering how Testa and Pigmeo had managed to become involved with the likes of Florenz Cull—or his twin, he reminded himself, having last seen the man lying at the bottom of a five-hundred-foot gorge in Yugoslavia some four years earlier.

The two didn't mix.

Cull was ruthless and inhumane, Testa and Pigmeo were soft-hearted; Cull was without the saving grace of emotional stability, while the odd couple was a maelstrom of conflicting ideals and isms carefully balanced by their infatuation with the rewards of the capitalistic process. He didn't think Arturo had ever killed a man in his life; Cull, on the other hand, had no room left on his gun for any more notches.

A puzzlement, he thought as he finished, shaved, and dressed. And of course, a puzzlement I shall not involve myself with because I am still on vacation and no one will bother me again—though perhaps Testa might return for the cash he slipped into a money belt at his waist.

A check of the mirror to be sure he was presentable, and he strolled outside, took a deep breath of air that he thought should be bottled and sold for a fortune in New York, and headed for the general store.

Aunt May was on the porch, sweeping and humming Confederate Civil War tunes to herself, and he could hear Owen behind the building, singing as he slung an ax against a defenseless tree stump. Lincoln waved, and Aunt May paused long enough to give him a mock curtsy and hand him the bill, whose size made him blanch.

"The cabin," she said.

"Ah."

"That's under the miscellaneous."

"All right." He checked the figure again. "You planning to replace it with a Hilton?"

"Materials are expensive these days, Mr. Black-thorne."

"May," he said, "you have a zillion trees right in your own backyard, for heaven's sake."

"Labor's outta sight."

"Owen works for free."

She sighed and leaned heavily on the broom. "An old woman's gotta plan for her retirement, y'know. Ain't right I should make exceptions for customers, even if they are pretty."

He smiled at the compliment, paid the bill in cash, and was rewarded with a brown paper bag in which, the woman said, she had packed a small lunch in case he wanted to stop on the way. He thanked her until he saw the lunch included on the tab, then shook his head and walked into the store, bought a suitcase and extra clothes, and left. Then he walked around to the back, where his rented car was parked. A word with Owen, who'd seen nothing unusual since dawn, and he tossed his belongings into the backseat, slid in behind the wheel, and fired the ignition.

"You be back?" Owen asked.

Lincoln shrugged. "Depends on when May finishes the hotel."

The young man nodded sagely. "Gonna be a beaut when it's done, mark my words."

"I expect a plaque somewhere with my name on it as chief donor to the charity."

Kintab laughed and stepped away as Lincoln gave him a salute and drove off slowly, trying not to kick up too much dust on the clothes hanging on the line, or on May, who was waving his money at him from the porch. He waved back, bumped onto the road, and headed east into the forest. A quick calculation had him into Bangor the following morning, on the plane to Boston by late afternoon, and home in New Jersey the day after that. He was in no hurry to return to work. What he wanted most now was a leisurely drive through some of the most beautiful country on the continent, a stay at a motel or two along the way, and more rich food than he knew was good for him.

A muffled thumping sound behind and under the car made him scowl and hurriedly check the gauges arrayed on either side of the steering wheel. Then he checked the road ahead for depressions and potholes, or rocks spilled onto the blacktop from the slopes on either side.

Wonderful, he thought as the thumping continued; I'll break down in the middle of nowhere, it'll take me a month to hitchhike to civilization, and I'll bet a million bucks I'll still never see a damned moose.

The road climbed easily, dropped sharply, swerved without guardrails on curves that overlooked pocket valleys almost picture postcard-perfect. There was no sign of tourists, or hunters, or even small towns. The silence was perfect, the air filled with the sharp scent of pine, and after the first hour the thumping stopped, and he slowed down, relieved there was nothing wrong and realizing he was in no hurry to get anywhere, much less an airport.

An unconscious touch of his hand to the money belt made him wonder a bit about the Viking statuette and what it meant, but he decided that Arturo would contact him soon enough once he reached home. This kind of money was not going to be a gift from the gods.

By noon the rugged mountains had degenerated into high hills, and there were increasingly distressing signs that other motorists were on the road with him; they passed him at twice the speed, they filled the verge with beer cans and bottles, and they glared and made unkind gestures when he refused to do more than the legal limit. It was a portent, he concluded, that not one of them was from Maine.

Shortly after one, he pulled over to a designated picnic area, which was little more than a widened clearing off the highway and four round redwood tables, and a trashcan with a picture of a moose on its side. He stretched the miles from his legs and arms, and sat on the nearest bench. In the bag were four thick sandwiches made from homebaked bread, and a Thermos of lemonade, and he made the most of the meal, humming to himself and listening to the birds until, just as he'd started the last sandwich, he heard one of the birds thumping. He looked up, thinking it might be a woodpecker. He looked around, thinking it might be a bear trying to knock down a tree.

Then he looked at the car and saw it rocking on its wheels.

Haunted, he thought.

The thumping grew louder, and for a moment his heart paused—he was almost sure he heard a voice calling.

The thumping stopped, and the car came to rest,

and he looked at the sandwich with gloom in his eyes.

"I am not going to open the trunk," he insisted as he rose and pulled the keys from his hip pocket. "I am not going to do it because it is not a moose in there."

A sniff, a brush of his hand through brown hair dropping over his forehead, and he walked over to the car, stood staring at the trunk, and felt like an idiot when he said, loudly, "Is anyone in there?"

A thump gave him the answer.

"Hell."

A search of the ground found him a good-sized rock he hefted once or twice. Then he inserted the key, turned it, and flung up the lid as he jumped back.

"My god!" a woman said, squinting up at the light. "Are you deaf?"

"If I'm not being impertinent, who the hell are you?" he answered.

She shook her head to keep him silent for a moment, and climbed stiffly out, placed her hands in the small of her back and rocked side to side, groaning, then moaning into a brisk series of deep knee-bends. A dozen jumping jacks. A half-dozen side kicks. Then she reached into the trunk, pulled out a knapsack and from it extracted a brush she ran through shoulder-length hair the deepest shade of honey.

Lincoln dropped the rock and watched her, watched how the material of her plaid shirt stretched over her torso while the material of her jeans did not stretch as much as flowed over her

41

hips and legs. Her eyes, when she finally paused long enough to look at him and grin, were dark blue, her nose sharp, her mouth small and naturally red.

Well, he thought, if I can't have a moose.

The sound of a large truck rumbled from around the near bend in the road.

"Who," he said, "are you?"

"Molly Partridge," she answered, offering her hand for him to shake.

The truck grew nearer.

"Okay. What were you doing in my trunk?"

"It's a long story."

"How long?"

She shrugged. "Depends on how much you want to hear."

The truck lumbered around the bend. Lincoln looked up over the roof of the car and saw it—a milk tanker, its aluminum sides gleaming in the sun, the windshield blanked by the shadows of the trees whipping across it.

Molly turned when she saw she had lost his attention. "Big one," she noted. "God, he must be doing—"

The truck reached the straightaway, corrected itself, and its engine roared as it barreled right for them.

"Hey!" the woman shouted.

But the driver didn't listen. Instead, he plowed his high-grilled vehicle straight into the front of Lincoln's rented car.

FIVE

LINCOLN GRABBED MOLLY'S ARM AND YANKED HER out of the way, both of them running nearly backward toward the tables, his free hand up to protect his face from the dirt and rocks showered onto them from the truck's massive tires.

The car's windows shattered instantly on impact, the hood folded and rose, and the vehicle itself was slammed backward, slewing side-on into the trees as the truck turned back to the road and roared off, its gears shrieking, the tanker swinging from side to side as the wheels sought and found purchase.

A moment later it was gone, the sound of its rumbling fading like distant thunder.

Molly dropped immediately onto a bench and began trembling, covering her face with her hands while Lincoln looked at the car, then walked to the road and looked west. He could smell gasoline, burnt rubber, and hot metal, and his nose wrinkled as he turned back and sat opposite the woman he had found in the trunk.

"You know the milkman?" he asked.

Her hands lowered, and she shook her head.

That, he figured, was about par for the course.

"It always happens, you know," he said, more to the trees than to her. "Somebody always wants me to do something that I don't want to do. Then they give the idea to someone else that I'm going to do it, and someone else who doesn't want me to do it tries to see that I don't do what I'm not doing. Which, quite naturally, makes me a little stupid because then I want to do it, even though in this case, I haven't a clue as to what I'm supposed to do."

Molly looked at him from behind a curtain of hair. "What?"

"It made perfect sense to me." He watched her closely and saw she wasn't as hurt as she was frightened. "And you don't have any idea who that was?"

"I already said no."

"Then would you tell me what you were doing in the trunk?"

They both looked over at the car, and suddenly she gasped at the realization that if Lincoln hadn't opened the lid when he had, she'd now be a part of the twisted, smoking metal canted against a trio of stout, scorched pines.

Lincoln waited patiently until the reaction had passed before asking again for an explanation.

"I needed a ride to Bangor," she said, blowing the hair out of her eyes.

"In a trunk?"

"I didn't know if you picked up hitchhikers."

"I don't."

"See?" Her smile was tremulous. "I figured that if I stowed away until you were on the road, you wouldn't leave me out here in the middle of nowhere."

Lincoln allowed as how that was probably true. "But how did you get in there in the first place, especially without any of the Kintabs seeing you?"

"I picked the lock." She reached for her knapsack, rummaged a bit, and pulled out a small leather case. When she opened it he saw a mint condition set of locksmith tools. Softly, he whistled his admiration, and this time her smile was more confident. "I waited until just before dawn, then got in. I thought," she said with a hint of accusation, "you'd want to get an early start."

"I was tired."

"I was cramped."

His head tilted to one side, listening to the calls of the forest. He thought he heard the truck again. When Molly said nothing, however, he put it to an echo of the attack, and redirected his attention.

"How did you get out here? It's not the most populated or popular place in the state."

"I was hiking."

His look was skeptical. "Out here?"

"I like Maine."

A finger pointed at the toolcase. "You were hoping to open the secrets of Nature?"

"I like to be prepared," she told him huffily. "And if you're not going to give me a ride, I'll just have to—"

The roaring.

They jerked around just as the milk tanker bellowed around the far bend, its chimney exhaust belching black smoke, its high chrome grille flaring darts of sunlight into their eyes.

Molly was already on her feet and heading for the

trees, shouting for Lincoln to follow her before it was too late, but he only stood and waited, thinking the driver would have to brake soon or he'd smash himself and his vehicle into the nearest trunk. Besides, he wanted a look at whoever was trying to turn him into tire tracks.

He was wrong.

The moment the tanker hit the verge, the driver heaved the wheel over, and the tank began to slide, spewing dirt and rocks like missiles again, its rounded back end aiming at the tables, and at him.

But instead of running, Linc raced for the bucking cab, paying no heed to the explosive splintering of wood as the tank smashed into the tables and benches, sending the latter pinwheeling into the air, and the planks of the former into propellers that lashed at the foliage and showered the ground with branches. Something large thudded painfully against his back and nearly cost him his footing, but he leapt for the running board, one hand grabbing the outside mirror as the cab's wheels caught the blacktop while the driver fought to bring the rest of the rig under control and move away from his charge.

The passenger door window was darkly tinted, and when he yanked frantically on the handle he cursed when he found it was locked. But before he jumped free he managed to press his face to the glass and see a large man scowling at him. There were too many shadows and not enough time, yet he was able to note that the man was wearing a brightly colored flowered shirt that was tight on a chest too large to be real.

He pushed himself away as the tanker growled through its gears, landing in a roll on the weedy verge. By the time he had regained his feet, the truck was gone.

So was Molly Partridge.

He searched the nearby woodland for over an hour, calling, thinking at first she had been injured in her flight, then thinking she just might be too frightened to show herself until she was positive the danger was over. But the truck didn't return, and neither did she, and he decided he wasn't going to wait around for one or the other. A check of the totaled automobile found his suitcase reasonably intact, and after wrapping a cord of ground ivy around it, he started east again.

Within the next sixty minutes, eight vehicles passed him, and none even slowed down when he stuck out his thumb; the following thirty minutes saw ten more, but only one of them even hesitated before speeding up and coating him with dust. He supposed he didn't look all that respectable, what with the dirt and sweat staining his clothes, the ivy-tied suitcase dangling from his hand, and his hair plastered to his skull by the warm afternoon sun; on the other hand, his smile was certainly friendly enough, and his face was anything but menacing, so what was wrong with these people that they wouldn't assist a fellow human being in obvious unfortunate circumstances?

A fork in the road precipitated a silent debate, an imaginary toss of a coin, and a veering to the right.

No one came by.

No one wanted to help him.

A sad commentary on contemporary life, he thought as he crested a hill and stopped. The suitcase had gained forty pounds in the last ten minutes, and he was tempted to check to see if Molly had hidden herself inside; his legs were stiffening, and there were invisible pebbles digging into his boots; and the plank fragment that had cracked across his back had left behind a bruise now threatening to make his spine permanently rigid.

He sighed, and looked at the incredibly steep slope ahead of him, at the boulder on the side of the road, and chose the latter to perch on and rest a while. It wasn't easy getting to the top, but he made it, drew his knees to his chest and looked at his destination.

A small town on a broad river. Smokestacks from mills and factories. Though the colors of the houses he could see might have been bright, from here they had taken on a dingy cast, almost as though he were seeing them through a smoky twilight. He had no idea what the name of the place was, but he was sure that it was a town young people grew up in to leave, even if they had to use shoe leather to do it.

His legs parted a bit, and he looked down between his knees to the slope of the rock, and what he hadn't seen before—that the hillside became a cliff immediately beyond his shadow, and the drop looked to be at least two hundred feet.

His stomach contracted, his brow felt sheathed with ice, and he backed slowly away. Heights, the acceptance thereof, and the consequences of falling off were not his forte; he did not fancy the feeling of sublime euphoria that overcame him when standing on the edge of a precipice—the feeling that he really could fly if he just leaned forward a little and let himself fall. He was, after all, immortal, and the trip to the bottom would be no more trouble than sailing on a down pillow.

Once on solid ground again, he checked the road, the position of the sun in the sky, and started down, his thighs instantly protesting the angle and the weight put on them so he wouldn't roll to the flat below. His suitcase thumped against his leg, his head filled with a faint dizziness, and he was forced to stop several times to wipe the perspiration from his eyes.

Midway down he glanced over to his right and saw another road, one considerably less steep, and filled with traffic. His lips twisted in disgust. No wonder he hadn't seen anyone here; they all used the other way. When he looked back, he saw that the hill he was descending was actually a narrow pillar of land that no one in his right mind would want to climb out of choice.

"Great," he muttered, and continued on down, reached the flat and walked to the first intersection, on all sides of which were small open fields barren of crops and gouged with trenches into which garbage had been bulldozed.

He dropped the suitcase and sat on it, propped his elbow on his leg and poked out his thumb. Every few minutes he changed its direction, not particularly caring where he went as long as he didn't have to walk there.

No one stopped.

The sun reached the top of the hills behind him,

and he began to feel chilled as the perspiration dried on his skin under the urging of a breeze escaping from the dark woods on the slopes.

By the time the first automobile had gone by with its running lights on, he had decided there was no future in playing signpost to oblivion. He rose, groaned at the sudden stabs of pain in his limbs and back, and started for town. Turned around and picked up his suitcase, and started off again. At least, he thought, he wouldn't want for a decent meal or a bed. All he had to do was find a motel, a hotel, a boardinghouse, a chicken coop for crying out loud, plunk down a twenty and get waited on.

Only once did he consider sleeping in the garbage dump—when he saw a highly polished milk tanker lumbering toward him. He went through seven different contingency plans before he realized that the glass wasn't tinted, that there were markings on the side, and that the driver, when he shot past with a puzzled frown in Linc's direction, wasn't wearing a Hawaiian Rorschach shirt.

Suddenly, the tailor shop in Inverness didn't seem quite as drab as he'd thought the day before.

Thirty minutes later he found himself at the river, standing in front of a block-long series of buildings weathered brown, high windows streaked when they weren't broken, all facing a disintegrating street that followed the water's meandering course. He counted three bars, a small grocery-and-liquor store, and at the far corner what apparently, for this neighborhood, passed for a hotel.

Inside, the lobby was musty, dimly lighted, and the front desk was in an alcove to his left. Behind it sat an old, bald man in shirtsleeves reading a one-volume encyclopedia. Lincoln walked up to him, cleared his throat, rang the bell, and smiled his best when the clerk looked up, scowling.

"Did ya know," the old man squeaked, "that the English, in the old days, used to use sheep intestines for condoms?"

Lincoln put down the suitcase.

"Fact."

He nodded, reached for a registration card and began filling it out with a fountain pen he plucked from a carved wooden holder.

"Bet ya didn't know that the redskins didn't have horses until the Spanish brought em over."

Lincoln pulled a twenty from his pocket and laid it on the counter.

The old man closed the book, reached behind him and grabbed a key. He peered at the number, and tossed it to Linc, who snatched it out of the air and nodded his thanks.

"No wine, no women, no song," the old man cautioned as Linc headed for the stairs.

"You're no fun," he said.

"I got my standards," was the reply. "Room service closes at four."

He was impressed.

"An hour ago."

He took the stairs heavily, noting the peeling linoleum, the thin railing slick from use, the hanging lights overhead with white globes dusty and lined with cracks. At the second floor landing he pushed through a door into a narrow, green-carpeted hallway. His room was at the front. River view. One bed with a mattress thin enough to be a rug, one pillow lumpy enough to be an egg carton, and a matching sheet and army blanket. The dresser had two of its three drawers missing. The chair by the high window only had three legs. The musty bathroom was closet small, all the porcelain stained, the water tepid, the shower not working on more than one cylinder.

He washed, stood under the shower for nearly twenty minutes, and walked out with a towel wrapped around his waist.

He stood to one side of the window and looked out, holding aside the dreary white curtain with one hand while the other fought to keep the towel in place.

The street below was filling slowly with pedestrian traffic; refugees, he thought, from the yard at Sing Sing. A pair of women wandered by, unaccompanied and trucker-tough. On the water an empty barge was shoved eastward by a tugboat. Across the water a hill sloped steeply upward, streets dug into it, houses clinging precariously to the curbs. There were no docks that he could see on either bank, but a handful of rowboats were tied to makeshift moorings driven into the graveled ground in front of his block.

There was a man in one, he saw when the streetlamps flared on. A short man incongruously carrying a bow and arrow. Lincoln figured him for a hunter who disdained modern weaponry, then knew he was wrong when the man suddenly straightened, looked right at him, and fired an arrow at his heart.

SIX

THE WINDOW SCREEN, WHAT THERE WAS OF IT, parted without a sound, then the arrow burst through, but the door shook as if it had been thumped by a giant when the missile embedded itself a good two inches into the old, thick wood; and the shaft vibrated so rapidly it hummed for several seconds.

Lincoln, who had thrown himself wildly to one side immediately he saw the release of the string, took his pulse and checked his chest for unwanted intrusions, then rose cautiously and peered out from behind the curtain. The man was gone, already making for the center of the river and rowing eastward as rapidly as he could—a dark, menacing figure oddly marked by the brilliant green Hawaiian shirt he was wearing.

No one on the street seemed to notice a thing; the five male pedestrians he could spot were busily negotiating brief visitation rights with the two women he had noted strolling the riverbank earlier. If they had seen or heard the attack, they were used to it, perhaps believing it was merely part of the local color provided for their evening's entertainment.

In any case, none of them bothered to look up at the window, or look out at the river where the oarsman was already vanishing into darkness.

Lincoln shivered and hugged himself as he straightened; he shivered more violently when he looked down and realized that the arrow had been somewhat low, and more close to its target than he'd realized.

He was naked.

He looked to the door, saw the arrow, and saw his bath towel dangling from it; it was all he could do to keep from crossing his legs.

Then, as he sidled along the wall toward the dresser and snatched up his shorts and jeans, he saw a piece of paper wrapped around the arrow's shaft. An eyebrow arched. He switched off the overhead light in case his assailant had a partner, and tugged the arrow from the door—not without a certain amount of difficulty since, when he finally freed it, he saw that the steel tip was doubly barbed.

Slowly, then, he backed into the bathroom, pulled down the ratty shade and sat cross-legged in the corner on tiles that were nearly slick with ill-cleaning. He examined the missile closely, discovered no distinguishing marks except for the towel, and finally unwrapped the paper, tilted it toward the light over the sink, and arched his other eyebrow.

You, it said in the most delicate script he had ever seen outside a monastery in northern Czechoslovakia, *are not appreciated here. You are not wanted here. You are not required to be here. You are not needed here. You will go back where you came from.*

You will go home to New Jersey. You will make your cheap suits and you will live a long and peaceful life.

It was unsigned, and he read it twice more before deciding there was no code involved, just a simple, straightforward warning to get out of town. Assuming it wasn't a local policeman who had seen too many westerns, then it had to be Florenz Cull, or whatever passed for the man these days. And if that was the case, then he had no intention of disobeying.

But, he thought as he struggled to his feet and returned to the bedroom, if I do what he says, I'll never be able to look at myself in the mirror again.

He scowled at the dilemma, dropped the note on the bed, and turned to the dusty mirror over the dresser. He peered at his reflection, leaned close, leaned away. He crossed his eyes, thumbed his nose, and concluded that not looking at himself in the mirror again was a crock, especially since he was the only man he knew who could cut himself shaving with an electric razor. Not using a mirror, then, would be suicidal.

Still, he did not cotton to the comment about his tailoring abilities. His suits, his dresses, his shirts, his ties, and whatever else the customer desired, were carefully crafted and always lasted far longer than the fashions they copied, unless the purchaser was beyond fashion, which most of them who could afford him were. He had never had a return for dissatisfaction.

He dressed slowly, turned out all the lights, bolted the door and the window, and sighed when he realized there was no air-conditioning unit in the place. With much contortion, then, to keep out of the line of fire of any other Hawaiian hunters in the area, he lowered the top window an inch, raised the bottom one two, and stretched out on the bed, hands clasped behind his head.

He was going to sleep.

Tomorrow, after he found a breakfast decent or not, he would decide whether he should accept the insult and the warning as they were intended, or tell the sender to find a swift chute to hell and see if he couldn't locate Arturo.

He needn't have bothered to worry himself.

When he awoke the next morning, shortly after dawn, Salome Testa was lying beside him in her snug silk dress, a curiously dreamy smile on her moist red lips.

After considering the various and enlivening possibilities he might not have been aware of while he had slept, he leapt from the bed as if he'd been stung and snatched up the arrow from the wastebasket where he'd tossed it. He held it defensively in front of him and cleared his throat loudly, four or five times, until she woke up.

"Ah," she said, stretching disconcertingly and pushing herself back until she was sitting against the headboard.

"Ah yourself," he said. "How did you get in?"

"The door was open."

"No, it wasn't. I locked it before I went to bed."

She held up a key magically produced from the slope of her neckline. "It was eventually open."

"Ah."

"So I have said."

"Where's the shrimp?"

"In Pittsburgh."

"Good place for him." After careful visual examination, he was satisfied there was no place she could have hidden a weapon, so he dropped the arrow on the dresser behind him, and crossed his arms over his chest. "Now. An explanation."

"You have my money."

He nodded; so far so good.

"I would like it back."

"I thought you wanted me to find some kind of statuette, that Viking fella."

She pursed her lips, closed one eye, and fluffed her long red hair back into place. One long-fingered hand began smoothing the wrinkles from the silk over her legs. The eye opened. "I thought you were not interested."

"Someone blew up my vacation, so to speak."

"So I heard."

"You didn't by any chance see who did it?"

"A little fat man with a funny shirt."

He nodded. "I am no longer surprised." A hitch of his belt, and he narrowed his eyes slightly. "I'm told that Florenz was in town just after you arrived."

She paled, blinked rapidly, and forgot to smooth the wrinkles that had formed over her stomach. "You kid."

"I never kid about the dead."

"He is not dead."

"I gathered that." He pointed to the arrow, then to the ragged hole in the door. "His friend also totaled a rented car, which I am going to find awfully hard to explain to their front office."

Her gaze lowered.

He rubbed his neck. "It would be too much to ask, Salome, but I certainly hope Cull doesn't want that Viking as well."

Her gaze lifted.

"Oh hell."

"He is adamant."

"Nice."

"He told us he would not like it very well if we continued looking for the piece. He told us we would find this time of year more comfortable back in Milan."

"Ah. And when did he tell you all this?"

"Yesterday afternoon, before he took Arturo to Pittsburgh."

"All right." He picked up the arrow and rolled it between his palms, then crossed to the bed and sat down beside her. She did not move away, nor did she encourage intimacy; it was a difficult situation, but she maintained her poise. "I suppose it would be proper here to ask just what in hell is so important about that Viking that a thing like Florenz Cull wants it so badly."

"It is an artifact of great value," she said, turning her head just enough to show him both her eyes.

"He was never in his life interested in anything older than a month. Except women, of course, and I think they scare him. Besides, if that were true, every major museum in the world would be vying for it. A fortune could be made just at a private auction." He shook his head. "Cull doesn't need the money. And neither do you."

"I am frugal, it is true."

Her hand stopped smoothing the silk and drifted to his thigh.

"And you two don't live in one place long enough to have any collection at all."

"We are world travelers."

"I'll let that pass."

Her fingers squeezed, gently.

"You will not believe it when I tell you."

He knew, then, he should have gotten up, kissed her, grabbed his suitcase with the ivy wrapped around it, and walked out the door. Out of this town. Out of Maine.

Because he knew, once he heard it, he would believe it. He had seen too many things supposedly fantastic that were all too realistic; he had held in his hands too many items that should have been relegated to movies and books; and he had nearly been killed by too many all-too-living creatures that normally comprised the population of too many nightmares.

He should have left, and he didn't, because one of these days he wasn't going to believe, and then he'd be able to cut-and-snip without worrying, for the rest of his life.

"Do you want to hear?"

"No."

She pouted.

"Tell me."

"You changed your mind?"

"I didn't not want to hear in the first place."

"Then why say so?"

"To ease my conscience, so when I die I can't say I didn't warn myself."

She searched his face for levity, found none, and frowned. "You are very strange."

"Tailors get like that when they get shot naked."

"Oh?" She smiled for the first time.

"It's a long story. Yours first."

She settled herself by wriggling her rump and fluffing her hair, checking her makeup in the mirror in the sequined purse at her side. Once done, the hand stopped its squeezing, and before he knew it he was listening to a voice honey-soft and laced with poison, telling him that the ferocious-looking Viking he had seen in the photograph was actually a wooden statuette fourteen inches high, expertly hand-carved and found in a deep snow-cave high in the mountains of northern Norway. The pair of government archeologists who discovered it in the early 1930s quite naturally thought they had come upon the site of a pagan place of worship maintained in secret long after Christianity had slipped into Scandinavian life. Whether they were correct or not was apparently beside the point, because the day after they brought it back to Oslo, they were found dead in their rooms, and the statuette gone. They left behind only a few fragments of notes, which disappeared within the month.

The rather unremarkable artifact was soon forgotten in the turmoil of the coming war, but evidently the notes resurfaced just before the conflict broke out. They indicated that the statuette was more than just a simple carving; they suggested, not without a dash of skepticism or an awed fear of belief, that behind the thick patch over the left eye of the warrior was a source of incredible, perhaps even supernatural, power.

The scientists, being scientists, laughed.

Hitler, who was just as crazy, did not. He was well-known to have been nearly fanatical about the realms of the occult, and among those who understood such things—as opposed to historians and politicians—it was believed that the subsequent invasion of Norway was carried out partially to recover the Odin Soldier, which is what it became known as, though no one knows why.

If that power source was real, Hitler would have his ultimate weapon; if it wasn't, he had lots of mountains, ice, and control of the North Sea.

As it was, he had heartburn, and it wasn't until last year that Arturo, in his earnest if not terribly skilled explorations of the world's museums and anonymous collectors, discovered by accident the photograph which, he cleverly deduced, was very recently made. Which meant someone had the Soldier, and might be even now tutoring himself in its use.

He took the others, for which Salome posed so fetchingly, in order to camouflage the one of the Soldier.

Apparently, he made a mistake.

Lincoln listened without comment, and when she was done, he rolled off the bed and stood at the window.

"You expect me to believe that?"

"The man who supposedly has this thing was in the state of your Washington a few years ago."

Sure, he thought; why not?

"And he was in Sicily not long ago."

Interesting speculation, he thought without turning.

"Arturo believes he was last heading for Hawaii."

"Now wait a minute," he said, at last losing control. "Are you trying to tell me that this guy—"

"His name is Montague Partridge."

"—is going around the world pulling the plug on —who?"

Salome blinked at the way he stared at her, and pulled her legs to her, gripping her knees and trying to push herself through the wall into the next room.

"Who did you say?"

She said "Montague Partridge" just as the door slammed open and an old man raced in, shotgun in hand, both barrels high and aiming at Lincoln.

"I said," the man declared, "no wine, no women."

And he pulled both triggers.

SEVEN

SALOME WHIMPERED AND COWERED AGAINST THE headboard; Lincoln just closed his eyes and waited for the pellets to shred his soul and the only clean shirt he had left. When nothing happened after several long heartbeats, however, they both opened their eyes just in time to see the desk clerk swear, break open the weapon and press two cartridges into the chambers. By the time Lincoln had the presence of mind to move, the barrels were up again and aiming at his chin.

"I don't suppose," Lincoln said, "it would do any good to say this isn't what it looks like, and it isn't my fault. That she came in here while I was asleep."

"Gentlemen, please, not on my account," Salome muttered, readjusting her skirt and puckering her lips.

"Nope," the desk clerk said. The shotgun was somewhat too heavy for his scrawny arms, but he managed to steady it long enough to gesture the woman off the bed and into the chair beside the window. Then he sniffed, readjusted the shotgun in his grip, and backed toward the door.

"You," he said to Lincoln, "come with me."

"I don't see anything wrong with that," he said, smiled an apology to Salome and picked up his suitcase. The old man backed slowly out of the room, Lincoln following, until they were clear of the threshold. Then the old man called out to Salome that she should follow them at a distance of ten paces and don't try anything otherwise her boyfriend was going to become part of the Sunday buffet.

Lincoln wasn't sure he understood the logic behind all this, but as long as the old man was holding the trigger, and the hallway was too narrow to make a move, he wasn't about to argue. So he continued moving toward the retreating desk clerk, hearing Salome grumble as she followed. Somewhere down the hall a door opened and shut very quickly; behind them another door opened, and Lincoln wondered at the clientele's capacity for noninvolvement until he heard what sounded like an off-key Westminster chime. Despite himself and the shotgun, he turned around and saw Salome slumping slowly to the floor. Standing behind her was Molly Partridge and her nonmusical skillet.

She grinned, dropped the skillet and dragged Salome back into the room.

Lincoln looked to the old man, who had lowered the gun and was already trudging wearily toward the staircase. Heads or tails, he thought, and decided the old man was safer.

Down in the lobby, the clerk slumped into his chair behind the alcove counter and mopped his face with an oversized handkerchief, reached under his seat and pulled out a flask which he opened, drank from, coughed over, and closed again before replacing.

"Did you know," he said, "that the Mongols used to cook their meat by puttin it under their saddles and riding on it all day?"

"No," Lincoln said, "and what the hell is going on around here?"

The old man extended his hand. "Cleveland Ash," he said. "Folks around here call me 'Prez' on account of the first name."

Lincoln hesitated, took the offer, and widened his eyes when he felt the strength in fingers that looked less substantial than a tubercular chicken's legs. "I don't suppose you want to tell me what's going on here."

"I don't know," Ash said. "I'm just doing what I'm told."

"What? You mean you work for that woman?" he said, turning to watch Molly take the stairs down two at a time.

"Nope. Just took a bribe, that's all." He squinted a look of disbelief. "You mean, you ain't never bribed a desk clerk in your whole life?"

"Not so it took."

"Get a fatter wallet."

Molly bounded up to them then, grinned at Ash and blew him a kiss he accepted with a nod and a wink. Then she took Lincoln's hand and led him out of the hotel onto the pavement. When she started across the street he balked.

"Hold it," he said. "Just hold it a goddamned minute."

"Boy," she said, "you aren't very appreciative."

I've missed something, he thought.

"Of what? I wasn't in danger, for god's sake, so you sure weren't rescuing me."

She grinned, and tugged at him until he either moved or fell into the gutter. Once on the other side, they headed for a small motorboat bobbing on a tether.

He balked again.

And Salome started screaming.

"Damn," said Molly, "I forgot the gag."

People began gathering in the street under the window from which the screams came. A few gestured toward the pair climbing into the boat, and Lincoln decided that the crowd, not being the most genteel he had ever seen in his life, was sufficient reason to play along with Partridge for a few minutes longer.

Especially when, as soon as the engine caught, the hotel blew up.

The explosion wasn't much as such things go, but it was sufficient unto the destruction thereof: most of the streetside windows blew out, flames spouted impressively from the roof, and the crowd dispersed in hot pursuit of safety as a handful of people came charging out the front door, slapping at their clothes and shouting for the medics. Debris showered blackly onto the street, the river, and the boat. As Molly busied herself aiming the bow into the middle of the river, Lincoln sought burning embers and either kicked or prodded them gingerly over the side. They heard sirens, what sounded like a few gunshots, and an ominous rumbling. He looked, and saw as if in slow motion the hotel's facade collapse, one story at a time, until there was little left in its space but a pile of smoldering rubble; the building to its left was afire, and he could see the rooftop of the third building puffing dirty gray smoke.

"That," he said, "must have been a hell of a bribe."

"I didn't do it," Molly said in a small voice as she turned the speed to full and swept east out of town.

"You didn't do what?"

"I didn't blow the building up."

He nodded, watched the fire a bit more, then turned to look over the bow, narrowing his eyes against the light spray that occasionally blew into his face. The air was warm, the water cold, and he couldn't help swallowing bile whenever he heard a new siren racing for the waterfront.

The engine's growl and his disinclination to turn around prevented further conversation until they had skidded around a bend in the river and the town was out of sight. Another fifteen minutes and another bend, and they were instantly flanked by tall pines that cast wavering black shadows on the water. He was shivering in spite of the August sun, and didn't object when the engine revved down and they headed for a small clearing on the riverbank's south side. The land sloped sharply upward for a hundred yards, and at the top he could see a van parked in front of a stout wood railing. The engine cut out, and the boat coasted to shore. He braced himself and leapt out just before the hull scraped bottom. He turned and pulled while Molly opened the casing and yanked at a few wires. When she was finished, she joined him and they hurried up to the road above.

Once in the van, Molly gripped the steering wheel tightly, but she made no move to slip the key into the ignition. Her face was pale, and she breathed shallowly, her mouth open to gulp for air. Lincoln could do nothing but watch until she calmed; and when she had, he touched her arm gently, to remind her he was there.

"I'm all right," she said at last. "Really I am."

"If you say so." He looked over his shoulder into the back, half expecting to see someone trussed up and gagged, but the space was empty save for a pile of old rags and tools. When he looked front again, she was already backing into the road. "You going to explain?"

"In a minute. Let me catch my breath."

"Excuse me, Miss Partridge," he said, "but I expect I already know a fair amount. Like about the Soldier, for example." He waited. There was no reaction. "What I'd like to know is why you went to so much trouble to find me again after running away like that."

"I was afraid."

"So was I."

"I didn't want to die. Not under a milk truck."

"Not exactly my primary death wish, either."

She smiled. "Then you understand."

This, he thought, wasn't going to get him anywhere.

Finally, Molly rolled her shoulders, grunted, stretched her arms full out and used the heels of her hands to steer them around the slopes of the hills. She hummed a bit, she chuckled once, and she took their speed up to something a little more than the legal limit in Germany. Ordinarily, he wasn't appalled by speed or by the careless concern drivers sometimes had for the lives and limbs of their passengers, but since the van had no discernible hood, and since the road therefore seemed to be vanishing directly under the soles of his boots, he found himself pressing back into his seat, one hand on the door handle in case ejection was necessary, the other gripping his thigh tightly.

"I didn't set that explosive," she said at last.

"You already told me that."

"You believe me?"

"Why would you bribe a clerk to get me out of my room and into the street if you wanted to blow me up?"

She frowned a moment. "I could have been trying to impress you with the seriousness of what I was doing."

"The shotgun was good enough, thanks."

"You're welcome."

They swerved in and out of a line of five cars, three of them overloaded station wagons that only barely gave them clearance; they ran a red light; they slammed over a one-lane bridge a headlamp ahead of an oncoming motorcycle.

"You know," Lincoln said, marvelling at the sound of his voice not breaking, "it would be faster using the interstate."

"Sure, but they would think that too."

He watched a cow in a pasture watch him glumly

as if he were soon going to be one of her leaves of grass. "Who," he said, "is they?"

"Oh, Cull, Molahu, those guys."

"I see. And I guess this has to do with the Odin Soldier."

"Well, sure it does!"

"I see. And I guess that your father knows something Cull wants to know. And who is Molahu, by the way?"

"Loop Molahu? A friend of Cull's."

They took a low rise without half bothering with the road, swept down into a shallow, narrow valley and into a small village where she stopped only long enough to fill the gas tank. Once on the road again, she headed more east than south, and the road widened into a four-lane highway that he discovered was no more immune to her banzai driving than the cowpaths. He suspected there'd be more.

Suddenly, he lost his temper.

He smacked the dashboard, slapped his leg, and faced Molly squarely. He might have growled a little; he definitely grunted loudly. When she saw his expression, she slowed and seemed to shrink a little in her seat.

"My father is dead," she whispered.

"I'm sorry."

"Oh, you don't have to be," she said brightly. "He died when I was a little girl, and my mother had to raise me and my brother on her own. I never knew him except for the pictures in the family album. Sad, I guess, but a lot of people never know their fathers, if you think about it. And it isn't all because they're dead, either."

"I'll think about it later." This woman, he thought as his temper struggled for dominance with his frustration, is going to be the death of me. "Then who is Montague Partridge?"

"My brother."

"Ah."

"He has the Soldier, you see."

"Ah. And he's currently in Hawaii, according to my late friend, Miss Testa. After having stirred the volcanic juices of two continents, if she's correct."

"Well . . . sort of."

The van took a pothole as if it were plunging into a gorge. Lincoln's head smacked against the roof, and several seconds passed before he was able to think clearly again.

"Salome wanted me to find the statuette, for money. I assume you want me to find the statuette for love."

"Oh no," she said, shaking her head vigorously. "Heavens no, I wouldn't do a thing like that. I mean, that's a little silly, don't you think?"

"Not as silly as all that. Countries have been lost because of love, you know."

She grimaced, thus placing that most romantic of notions into proper perspective. "Well, not this time, Mr. Blackthorne," she told him firmly. "This time we have to find it for the fate of the entire world!"

"Oh, for crying out loud."

The van slowed a bit more, so she could take her gaze off the road and stare at him earnestly. "I mean it!"

"You mean you're asking me to take on charity work?"

She blinked, checked the road to be sure they weren't aiming for a cliff, then looked at him again, aghast. "Are you serious? I mean, are you really and truly serious?"

He shrugged.

"You're serious," she decided.

"It doesn't really make much difference, does it," he said. "I seem to be in this affair whether I want to be or not, and all I ask for in my rapidly approaching old age is a straight answer to a very simple question—where in god's name are you taking me?"

"To the airport."

"Oh. To catch a plane, I suppose."

"Well, how else are we going to get to Hawaii?"

"How else? We can drive to Los Angeles or San Diego and get on a boat, that's how else."

"It'd be too late."

"For what?" He held up a hand. "No, never mind. Too late to save the world."

She nodded once, sharply, then suddenly jammed her foot onto the accelerator, shoving Lincoln back into his seat with an oath that made her blush.

"What . . . ?"

She pointed to the righthand outside mirror, and when he angled himself so he could see behind the van, he groaned.

Just as the milk tanker rammed into the rear bumper.

EIGHT

UNDER THE IMPACT, LESS HARSH THAN IT MIGHT have been, the van catapulted forward, skidded left onto the shoulder, and swung back again before the tanker could touch the bumper a second time. Molly, grim-faced and white-knuckled, glared at the highway and ignored the speedometer's rapid climb toward the engine's theoretical limit. She was too intent on both avoiding the truck and trying not to climb the backs of the few vehicles which began to appear in front of her.

Lincoln, feeling angrily helpless, just braced a hand against the dashboard, watching the image of the tanker in the mirror close the gap again, then drop slowly away as the highway rose steeply. It was little more than a temporary respite, but he used it to touch Molly reassuringly on the shoulder before climbing into the back. The junk pile he had seen there before had been scattered by the collision, and he looked frantically for something he could use as the van reached the crest of the knoll and plunged downhill. He was toppled onto his side as he reached for one of the rags, and landed with an oath on a tire iron and a claw hammer. The latter he kicked aside before it could puncture his leg; the former he snatched up and hefted, then crawled to the rear just in time to see the tanker slam into them again.

He was flung forward by the impact, barely getting a hand out in time to prevent him from cracking open his forehead. As it was, his arm protested, his knees protested, and he fell again as Molly swung back into the other lane. The tanker followed. Linc tried to see through its windshield, but the sun's light glared back in lances, and he could only guess that it was another one of the Hawaiian shirts, perhaps the same one that had played William Tell with his towel.

The angle of the road leveled and Molly muttered something angrily about people getting in her way when she was in a hurry. He didn't look forward; he didn't want to see who was stupid enough to try crossing a highway when two vehicles propelled by two equally mad drivers were looking for ways to add notches to their bumpers.

She muttered again at another car, which didn't seem to want to stay in its lane. Lincoln didn't blame it.

"Mr. Blackthorne," she shouted suddenly, "hang on! I'm going to try something!"

Alarmed, he turned to see what possible insanity she had up her sleeve, and nearly strangled on a cry —the highway wasn't in front of them anymore. Instead, she had veered sharply left and had jumped the grassy island separating the highway's directions; after a harrowing moment's correction, she grinned as she barreled wrong-way against the western flow.

He heard the horns, imagined the screams, and closed his eyes when she streaked back across the island just shy of a collision with an abruptly indecisive motorcycle. A horn blared. Tires billowed smoke and shrieks. He bounced off the right wall into the left, rolled over the bare floor and came up grunting against the back of the driver's seat when she finally applied the brakes with admirable diligence.

"Cop," she said over her shoulder.

He saw the patrol car off to the right, patiently waiting under the inadequate cover of a stand of pines. The tanker slowed as well. Molly wiped her brow with a sleeve.

"I think we got him."

"With what, a cannon?"

"No, silly. I mean, as long as the cop is there, that creep won't dare try anything."

"I don't mean to question your judgement," he said in the process of regaining his heartbeat, "but suppose the cop stays in the trees."

"Oh."

"Right."

He did.

The truck began to weave its way through the increasing traffic, using its horn to clear a path.

"Mr. Blackthorne?"

"I'm thinking, I'm thinking."

"Well, hurry! I can't do this much longer!"

The tanker pulled into the left lane and crawled abreast of them, the glare from its aluminum sides making Molly squint. By the time they had gone a half-mile, only the width of the broken white lane separated them.

"Are you finished thinking yet?" she asked nervously.

The van drew ahead as they climbed another rise, then dropped behind when an empty school bus pulled out in front of them from a side road. The tanker shot forward, changed lanes and slowed. The school bus wavered, then pulled around to pass.

"Hey," she said delightedly, "now we're chasing him!"

"Wonderful. What are you going to do when we catch him?"

"But as long as he's in front of us," she said, "he can't run us off the road, right?"

"If we're lucky."

"Boy, are you a pessimist."

"Habit," he said, and climbed into his seat, still holding the iron and staring at it. There was a sudden temptation to grin then, and he succumbed to it. "Pass him," he said as he rolled down his window.

"What?"

"Pass him."

Molly took her gaze from the highway just long enough to gape before she shrugged and floored the accelerator again. Lincoln leaned back and away from the wind rushing at his face, his right arm cocked and ready across his chest.

"Mr. Blackthorne," Molly said doubtfully, "be careful with that thing."

"You're right," he apologized. "It's too dangerous to have around."

With that, and as they drew even with the tanker's cab, he whipped arm and hand around, and the tire iron spun toward the driver's window. They were moving too fast for him to see if it reached its mark, but the effect was the same—the tanker darted right as though the driver were trying to avoid the impact, darted left as he compensated to avoid smashing over a white metal barrier that ran along the shoulder, dove right again to avoid another school bus, dove left to avoid the trees, and finally gave up to sputter to a halt on the shoulder.

By that time the van was already climbing yet another rise, and when Lincoln looked back he could see the patrol car pulling up behind the truck.

"I think we're all right," he said, sagging in his seat.

"I hope so," she told him, "because I think we have a flat tire."

Lincoln wasted no time pulling Molly from the van as soon as she stopped on the verge. When she protested, he only reached in and grabbed his suitcase, took her hand and began pulling her along the road, his thumb out while he ordered her to look pathetic. She didn't understand, but she managed it without much effort, and within five minutes they were in the back of a pick-up and crossing into New Hampshire.

"Y'know," she said, cringing in a corner away from the wind, "that was a perfectly good recreational vehicle. It had a lot of miles on it."

"I suppose it was a gift from your brother," he said, hugging himself against the unexpected chill.

She nodded curtly.

"He'll understand."

She shook her head decisively.

He started to say something else, saw the sour expression on her face and changed his mind. Besides, to be heard, he would have had to shout, and shouting was against his nature unless it occurred in the direst of emergencies. As it was, he had to figure out why, if Montague Partridge really had this Odin Soldier in the Hawaiian Islands, there were people here in New England trying to kill him. He didn't have it, he didn't want it, and he didn't know where the man was, specifically, who did have it, and wanted it, and was obviously attempting to test its strength—if, indeed, the story were true.

He might have found an answer, or at least a clue to an answer, but in the middle of his musing he fell asleep, not waking until Molly jabbed at his shoulder.

His eyes opened instantly, blinked, and looked around.

"Where the hell are we?" he said.

She was already climbing stiffly over the side and paused only long enough to point to the tall buildings around them and say, "Boston."

"Oh, lovely," he grumbled, and winced when the shriek of an airliner's engines threatened to take off his head. He ducked instinctively and looked up, groaning when he saw the streaks of grime on the underbelly of a 747.

"Logan Airport," she elaborated as she helped him down to the tarmac.

"My favorite place."

She stared at him puzzledly for a moment, then went around the truck bed to thank the driver. When she returned, she held out her hand.

"What?"

"Forty bucks," she said.

"For what?"

"I had to give him forty bucks to take us here. He was going to Portsmouth."

The truck pulled away, showering him with dust, and he turned his back to it, and stopped.

"This," he said when she dropped his suitcase at his feet, "is a terminal."

"That's right." A look, then. "Hey, Mr. Blackthorne, are you afraid of flying or something?"

He smiled at her stiffly, thinking of the time he got a nosebleed when he stepped over a packet of airmail stamps. It was a miserable burden to be saddled with, but one he'd managed to control simply by avoiding overseas letters and airports like this. The problem was, avoidance wasn't always possible.

He took a deep breath and tried to appear undaunted. She only looked at him more strangely.

He brushed a hand through the shock of brown hair tumbling over his forehead, and stared at the electronic doors right in the eye. "I suppose there is a ticket counter inside that just might, if extraordinary luck is with us, be able to book us passage to Hawaii."

"Right again," she said, taking his hand and pulling him through the entrance. "Now let me do all the talking, okay? I know how to handle these people. You just stand here and look important."

He took stock of his rumpled, dusty clothes, of the ivy-bound suitcase, and rubbed a hand over his stubbled face. He figured he might pass for an eccentric millionaire but not much else, but did his best to appear impatient, worried, and self-confident while he looked over the arrival-departure screens bolted to the counter's overhang.

There was a silent cheer when he couldn't find Hawaii, and one of despair when he realized that they'd probably have to stop at Los Angeles or San Francisco first—and there were five of those flights listed already.

Molly returned, took his arm and led him away to a half-empty coffee shop, where she promised to treat him to a hamburger and fries. She talked the entire time, chatting about the renovations done since she'd last been here, about the odd-looking people scurrying toward their flights, about the grease on their neighbors' plates in which a microbiologist might discover his own version of research heaven. She didn't quiet down until he reached across the tiny table and clamped a palm over her mouth.

"In other words," he said, "you've got the tickets and we leave in an hour."

"Well, not quite."

He refused to consider hope.

"I did get the tickets."

"I knew it."

"But we don't leave for three hours."

"Okay."

"And there's a connecting flight we have to catch."

"Really? Oh well, LA is—"

She sniffed, and quite suddenly her eyes filled with tears. "No, not Los Angeles."

He leaned back and stared at her. "Oh?"

"New York."

"Okay."

"Then St. Louis."

"Okay."

"Then Denver, if we're not delayed. By the airlines, I mean, not those other guys."

He put his knuckles to his eyes and seriously considered an exotic form of suicide.

"Then Los Angeles."

"Sure."

"We arrive at ten o'clock."

He scratched his upper lip, behind one ear, along the side of his neck, and had a feeling the ivy was going to wilt before she finished.

"Tomorrow night."

A look at the huge clock positioned over the grille. "That's not too bad, all things considered."

"Their time."

"Molly—"

"I know. That's the day after tomorrow, our time."

He asked for an explanation, and she told him that considering their recent perilous adventure on the highway, she thought it would be a good thing to make the trip as complicated as she could, to throw off any possible attempts to stop them. He allowed her a smile of approval and a pat on her hand, and she relaxed just long enough to tell him that she also figured the three hours they had would be useful.

"Oh?"

"Sure," she said. "Then we can figure out a way to get rid of Loop."

"Loop," he said. Then he nodded—Loop Molahu, one of the men trying to stop them. And it took him a moment to realize that she wasn't talking about the man in hypothetical terms. When she stiffened, then, he looked over his shoulder and saw the man standing in the coffee shop entrance. In his left hand he carried a suitcase; in his right hand he carried a pineapple, which he tossed in Lincoln's direction.

Reflex had Lincoln's hands out to catch the fruit before it struck the table.

And reflex made him snap his hands back when he saw the fuse burning brightly above the leaves.

NINE

LOGAN AIRPORT'S CRACK SECURITY FORCES ARE NOT used to having explosive devices arrive in their midst in the form of a plant whose very name has been lent to hand-tossed weapons of an expanding nature; they much prefer to use their keen eyes and wits, the marvelous, open-ended screening devices at the entrances to the flight gates, the occasional frisk, and the sharp-nosed canines that spend most of their time in the baggage rooms.

A member of said force, then, enjoying his lunch break at a corner table, was rather disconcerted when Lincoln shouted a warning and Molly screamed for emphasis, and there was a general stampede toward the four exits. The security man leapt to his feet, and was tripped by a child being shoved along ahead of its wailing mother; he scrambled back to his feet, and was slammed against the wall by Miss Partridge, who was in pursuit of a corpulent but muscular-looking gentleman in a garish flowered shirt; he rebounded in time to be rudely grabbed by a scruffy-looking man claiming to be a tailor and pointing to a smoking pineapple resting comfortably in the middle of a recently vacated table.

The security man, whose name was Stanley Oberon, attempted to regain some of his dignity by shaking off the hand and dusting his uniform.

"Damnit," Lincoln snapped, pointing again, "that's a bomb, you idiot."

"Sir, I'm afraid you'll have to come with me," Oberon said sternly. "It is a felony to create unreasonable panic in a public place, especially here where we're trying to stop terrorism in its tracks, and teach those miscreants we are not a nation to be toyed with on the international revolutionary front, as it were."

Lincoln examined the man's thin, pale face closely, wondering if he were any relation to Molly. Then he threw up his hands in exasperation and raced back to the table, Oberon following, after closing his gaping mouth. Linc grabbed up the pineapple, vaulted the luncheon-meat counter, and dropped it into a sink. Oberon drew his gun. Lincoln turned on the taps and vaulted the counter again, dropping to the floor and pulling the security man down beside him.

"Sir!" Oberon protested.

Linc held his breath.

"Sir, this is going to go hard with you if you don't come quietly."

In response, Linc pinned his shoulder to the floor and told him to shut up.

Outside the coffee shop there were muffled screams, the sound of running feet, and shouts from a number of men who seemed to be heading in their direction.

A minute passed.

Oberon, not sure that this wasn't a hoax but not willing to take the chance because it was, after all, only a part-time job until he could catch up on his alimony and become solvent again, waited with his revolver pointed at the scruffy man's nose.

Another minute passed, and the terminal grew silent.

A third minute brought Linc to his feet. He looked disdainfully at the barrel wavering nervously in his face and rounded the counter to check on the bomb. Oberon followed closely and gasped when the scruffy man picked up a carving knife and carefully pruned away the sharp-thorned, stiff outer leaves of the fruit. Inside was a dark powdery substance out of which protruded a fuse.

"That's a bomb," Oberon said, astonishment widening his eyes.

"Exactly, officer. And if you hurry," Lincoln told him gently, "you might catch the man who threw it in here. I think he didn't like the food."

Oberon holstered his weapon without hesitation and ran off, ran back for a description and ran off again. Lincoln watched him through the glass wall, shook his head and picked up his suitcase. Five minutes later, as he wandered aimlessly through a bookstore, Molly came in, her honeyed hair disheveled, her blue eyes dark with anger.

"Got away," she said.

"Too bad." He picked up a spy novel—Nazis running amok with the ultimate weapon in northern

Greece shortly after the war. "Do you think this will put me to sleep?"

"He went into the men's room."

"You didn't follow him?"

"Mr. Blackthorne, that was a men's room he went into!"

"Molly, the man tried to blow us up."

"But there are limits, proprieties, boundaries of acceptable public behavior."

"Bombing someone is acceptable?"

"You don't understand."

She was right, and he didn't think the book would put him to sleep so he replaced it, and took her back to the coffee shop. It was empty and they still had ninety minutes to go before they had to check in at their flight. When no one showed up to serve them, he sighed resignedly at the burdens life dumped so unceremoniously on his none-too-broad shoulders and cooked three hamburgers on his own, garnished them liberally, and dropped a bill on the register.

Molly could only stare when he sat down to eat, but didn't long resist the meal. She did, however, resist asking what had happened to the pineapple—there was a fruit salad for dessert, which she forcefully, but politely, declined.

Stanley Oberon returned just as they were finishing.

"Sir," he said, with far more respect in his voice than when they'd first met, "I think you'd better come with me to the chief's office."

Lincoln shook his head.

"Sir, the chief wants to question you about the incident."

Lincoln shook his head again, and began working on his salad.

Oberon looked to Molly, was struck mute for several seconds by her disarranged beauty, and pulled up a chair, clearly intending to plead with Lincoln, through her, for reason and the future of his job in airport security. What he received was a portion of fruit salad which, since his lunch had been interrupted, he accepted with pleasure.

"I don't believe it," Molly said, throwing her napkin down on the table, though since it was paper it lacked some of the impact she'd intended.

"Believe what?" Lincoln asked innocently.

"You," she said, and pointed at the entrance where Molahu had stood, at the counter, at the sink, and finally at the salad.

"Sir," Oberon said, "I really must ask you to come with me."

"Why?"

The security man frowned. "Well . . . well, because of the bomb, sir."

Lincoln touched his lips with a napkin and smiled. "What bomb?"

Oberon pointed at the entrance, at the counter, at the sink, and looked suddenly and fearfully at his clean plate. "Oh, sir."

"Friend," Lincoln said as he rose, "I understand how working in a place like this can get to you. Why don't you find something new, like being a traffic cop?"

Oberon swallowed painfully, and rubbed a knuckle across his eyes.

Molly stalked out ahead of Lincoln and did not look back until they had passed through a clutch of uniformed, steely-eyed personnel at the security gate. Then she only glared when he drew up alongside her.

"Hey," he said, "I saved our lives, you know."

"Maybe. But you wanted me to . . ." She tossed her long hair in disgust, and found them a pair of contoured plastic seats to wait in for the boarding call. "You wanted me to go into a *men's* room!"

He refused to answer. And refused to look at her. Instead, he scanned the faces of their compatriots in aeronautical suicide and hoped that none of them were working for Florenz Cull. Molahu, he decided, would not dare show himself soon again, even if he had discovered which flight they were on. He had to admit that Molly's tangled pattern to the West Coast would probably be effective; he also had to admit that Cull probably didn't have the resources to cover all the Pacific departures to Hawaii. All in all, it seemed to be a fair assumption that they would arrive in Honolulu in one piece.

What happened after that, however, he didn't want to consider, not until he'd arrived and proved himself correct.

Lincoln had no idea what time his body thought it was, but the pilot told him, in a carefully cheerful tone, that they were cruising at an unconscionable altitude over St. Louis. Molly was in the seat beside him, reading a magazine.

"You know," he said quietly, "you haven't told me why you're so anxious to find your brother."

"To save the world," she said without looking at him.

"I know that part," he reminded her. "But why you? Why haven't you gone to whatever authorities are in charge of saving the world and told them about it?"

"Would you believe it if you were them?"

"I believe somebody thinks it's true. And so, I think, would the authorities."

She shoved the magazine into the pocket in the back of the seat ahead of her and turned her head slowly. "Well, you're wrong."

"And you still haven't answered my question."

"I sure did."

"Then I didn't like the answer."

"It wasn't multiple choice."

The plane dipped and he grabbed her hand tightly. Revulsion flickered over her face, and was replaced by a show of sympathy. "All right."

He waited.

"I want to save my own skin, too."

He waited.

"See, Monty—that's what I call him because he hates his full name—Monty thinks that I want to kill him. So he's tried to kill me a couple of times already."

"I see."

"No, you don't," she said, and turned on the overhead light so he could check her expression for truth. "He did that, see, because I tried to kill him first."

He held up a hand. "Give me a minute," he said. "I want to think about that."

The pilot, a different one but still managing to sound just as cheerful as the first (unless it was the second, since Lincoln had lost track somewhere over Minneapolis), announced that they would soon be heading over the wild and truly scenic deserts of Utah and Nevada. Lincoln did not look out the window. It was still an hour before dawn, and one dark desert was, to him, the same as another.

"Why," he said to Molly, "did you try to kill Monty? He's your brother, isn't he?"

"Sure. He's eight years and five days older than me. He didn't like my father, either."

"You told me you hardly knew your father."

"That's true. But I still didn't like him."

"You didn't kill him, did you?"

"Not hardly."

"But you tried to kill your brother."

"He wouldn't give me the Soldier, once I knew he had it."

"So?"

"So, he's crazy, that's so. If I had killed him, we wouldn't be in this mess."

"Ah. Then that's why we're being chased, right? Monty is trying to stop you from coming to get him and this statuette."

"No."

"Oh."

"You don't get it yet, do you?"

"I don't think so."

"Think about it."

Los Angeles, Lincoln thought, is a cliché of itself, yet of its ilk a somewhat beautiful city. But despite his distant appreciation of the freeways, houses, and untested earthquake-proof buildings below, he still gripped the armrests tightly when the stewardess cheerfully announced they would be landing in less than ten minutes, and would all passengers please comport themselves accordingly. Lincoln decided she didn't mean scream for joy, so he turned to Molly instead.

"What you're saying is this—you want to get the Soldier before Monty kills you, and before Cull kills me. Once you have the Soldier, Monty won't want to kill you anymore, only Cull will. Then Monty will try to get the Soldier back, wanting to kill me for helping you—unless you kill him first.

"Cull, of course, wants the Soldier for his own ends, which may or may not include killing me.

"Monty wants it to blow up a few volcanos.

"You want it to save your skin and the world.

"And I want it, now, so I can go home and mend a few shirts."

Molly, who had frowned during the entire explanation, opened her mouth, closed it, opened it again, closed it, and shook her head.

"No."

"Okay, then where did I go wrong?"

"Saving the world."

"Huh?"

"I lied about the part about saving the world."

"You don't want to save the world?"

She pointed at the yellow smog. "Would you?"

They disembarked and, since there was no baggage to claim, began what seemed like a ten-mile journey to their connecting flight. Lincoln assumed it was leaving from the same airport, but he couldn't be sure when he thought he caught a glimpse of San Diego out one of the windows.

"Molly," he said, "if you don't want to kill your brother anymore, and you don't want to save the world from destruction, and you do in fact want to get hold of the Soldier, what the hell is going on?"

"Cull," she said simply.

"Cull?"

"Sure. I want to kill him."

He stopped just as they reached the security gate for their airline. "Wait a minute."

She stopped as well, and smiled back at him.

"Molly—"

"He killed my father."

Oh hell, he thought, and dropped his suitcase in shock when Molly stepped through the security gate and screamed as a flare of brilliant blue electricity exploded from the frame and engulfed her.

TEN

"ARE YOU ALL RIGHT?"

"My hair is frizzed."

Lincoln, for all that he wanted to be a gentleman, could not deny the visual truth of Molly's declaration, though he had compassion enough not to mention that it was also coiled, sprung, wired, and generally bent wildly out of shape. The variety of its condition amazed him, but not so much as the fact that she was alive at all.

When he had seen the burst of electricity take her, only a moment passed before he had snatched up his suitcase and flung it at her with such force that she was propelled out of the scanning area to sprawl unmoving on the floor beyond. Someone screamed for a doctor. A quick-thinking guard pulled the plug on the detector, and the area was immediately sealed off by a team from airport security. Officer Oberon was one of the men who examined the lethal connections, but he said nothing when he saw Lincoln standing anxiously by watching a medic work on Molly; when Lincoln saw him, however, he pulled him aside, congratulated him on his transfer, and asked if he'd seen a man in a

Hawaiian shirt hanging around. Oberon denied a sighting. Lincoln thanked him, examined the gate himself, and hurried after the unconscious woman, who was being carted out of the airport by ambulance attendants.

That was four hours ago. Now the sun had set, and he was still not sure she was quite herself. There was, fortunately, no apparent internal damage, and the burns she had received were, miraculously, exceedingly minor. Nevertheless, she was being held for at least another twenty-four hours for observation, and nothing either of them could say would change her physician's mind.

"It's all for the best," Lincoln told her.

"No, it isn't," she said weakly. "It means they have another day to get to Monty."

"But they'll stay off our backs. We're out of the picture, for now."

She sighed, and shrugged as best she could.

"Besides, this will give us a chance to plan something more than just rushing into the volcano's mouth, in a manner of speaking."

Her head moved slowly on the pillow, her face pale, her eyes lacking their usual glow. "We've lost."

"Not yet," he said. "If it comes to it, I'll go myself."

"Over my dead body."

He gave her a reassuring smile, rose from his chair and stood at the window, looking down at the hospital courtyard. Until now he had been confused at all the players in this charade, angered at what he believed were deliberate deceptions on the part of too many people to get him involved, and determined to see the job through only because he couldn't think of any way to get out of it.

Now he didn't want to.

It was one thing to come after him, because he expected it, tailors in the acquisition game being what they were; but when the viciousness of the hunt and chase spilled over onto perfectly innocent people, then his ire was aroused and his dander inflated.

And he was not thinking only of Molly, but also of those people who might have used that device ahead of them. All it would have taken would have been one businessman in a hurry, or a child scurrying away from its mother. . . .

He bunched his hands into fists and leaned his knuckles on the windowsill, and didn't stop glaring into the night until he heard Molly whisper a name.

It wasn't his. He turned slowly, ready to spring at the throat of any intruder, and caught himself just as a white-coated intern bustled into the room, smiled once, and bent over the stricken girl.

Molly spoke again, and Lincoln moved to the side of the bed, staring until the man looked up and pointed a revolver at his chest.

"Well, Blackthorne," said Florenz Cull, "what a surprise."

He was a startlingly tall man, as close to seven feet as one could get without making a fuss. His remarkable white hair, a vast mass of it, was brushed straight back from a high and creased forehead; his right eye was deep-set and black, his left covered with a plain black patch that made him look less piratical than one-eyed; his thin nose was hooked, and below a thin-lipped mouth his chin was so small as to be nonexistent. In place of his two missing ears he wore red prosthetic devices from which thin wires ran to an amplifier tucked into his breast pocket. There was, on his left hand, a red silk glove.

Lincoln backed to the wall, leaned against it, crossed his ankles, and put his hands in his pockets. "Florenz," he said by way of greeting.

"Amazing, isn't it, Mr. Blackthorne, how we keep bumping into each other."

Lincoln nodded. "The last time, as I recall, you had been bumped over a cliff."

"Unfortunate, to be sure," Cull said, sitting on the edge of the mattress and patting Molly's hand. "Luckily, a few trees broke my fall before I was ushered into the Netherworld. I didn't realize it until later, of course, but I had paid the price of surviving." He touched briefly each of the electronic hearing devices, and his heavily freckled face darkened. "I have you to thank for these, Blackthorne."

"You're welcome," he said softly.

Cull lifted one eyebrow, then made a slight adjustment to his volume control. "And now we meet again."

"Indeed we do. And what, if you don't mind my asking, are you going to do about it?" Said softly, tonelessly, and with the faint hint of a smile.

Molly, who had been following the conversation with a great deal of puzzlement, shrank away from Cull's hand when he returned his attention to her and pressed two fingers against the side of her throat. A wild-eyed glance to Lincoln only had him press a finger of his own to his mouth.

"I believe," Cull said with an approving nod, "this young woman is able to travel."

"That's not what her doctor says," Linc whispered.

"What?"

"You heard me."

"Stop playing your silly games with me, Blackthorne," Cull ordered harshly. "I am not alone, in case you were thinking of attempting to overpower me and escape. My two best men are waiting in the hallway."

"Ah," he said. "The milkman and the archer."

Cull scowled. "They were fools."

"They missed."

"As I said, they were fools."

"Lincoln?" Molly gasped quietly.

"It's all right," he said. "Whitey here won't try anything drastic in a full hospital."

Cull rose abruptly, his arms rigid at his sides, his height intensified by the dim light in the room. "You are not to call me that, Blackthorne."

"Sorry."

Cull's red glove patted at his abundant hair. "This sweep, if you will, of snowlike protein is a direct legacy from my mother, and I, for one, will not have my mother, rest her soul, insulted by a common tailor."

Lincoln pushed himself indolently away from the wall and walked to the window. The man's mother, he recalled, had vanished when she refused to pass over a considerable fortune to her only son before she died. "Whatever you say, Florrie, but you're still not going to get away with whatever you're planning. If you do, Molly will scream."

"Let her," Cull responded confidently. "As I told you, my men are already outside, in proper disguise, ready to whisk us all off to a private clinic in the hills."

Lincoln didn't like the sound of that.

"Of course, we shan't be going there at all."

He didn't like the sound of that, either.

"My private plane is waiting at the airport. And you know full well our destination."

That bothered him considerably.

"My dear," Cull said to Molly, again taking his place on the edge of the bed, "wouldn't you like to be reunited with your brother?"

She shook her head.

Cull tsked and pursed his lips. "That's not the attitude I would expect from a devoted sibling."

She stuck out her tongue and told him, quietly, to go to hell.

Before Lincoln could move, the gun was pressed hard into the hollow of Molly's throat, and she gagged, closed her eyes, and moved her lips in what he could only assume was a prayer for deliverance.

"Enough," he said sharply.

Cull only turned his head, and smiled. "I don't really need her," he said, his voice sibilant, "but I thought it would help dissuade dear Montague from holding on to that which does not belong to him. You will say nothing else, Blackthorne, or I will pull the trigger."

Molly muttered something.

"What's that?" Cull asked impatiently. "What did you call me?"

Though intrigued himself, Lincoln never found out.

Molly immediately raised her head, buried a hand in Cull's hair and screamed—directly into his right ear. Cull screamed back, dropping the gun as he scrambled with both hands to turn down the volume. But not before Molly had bitten his nose, yanked on his wires, and screamed a second time.

Lincoln dove for the weapon just as the door burst inward and two white-jacketed attendants raced in. They froze when they saw Cull writhing on the bed, and Lincoln standing in the middle of the room, aiming the revolver at them.

The corpulent one in the brilliant green shirt, Loop Molahu, glowered helplessly; his compatriot, a lank and flat-nosed Eddie Takana, dropped instantly into a threatening martial arts stance, saw the folly of his ways when Linc pulled back the hammer, and straightened, muttering to himself in a colorful combination of Japanese, Hawaiian, and California English. They both knew the tailor, and he knew them as well—the last time he had seen them was in Yugoslavia with Cull, when he had bound them both to a boulder with ropes made of sheep gut, just before he'd dropped Cull over the cliff.

"Get up, Molly," he said when he was sure they weren't going to try anything foolish.

"But I've been electrocuted!"

"Get up!"

She pushed aside the sheets, backed along the

wall to the narrow closet and fetched out her clothes. Lincoln ordered the two men to turn around, which they reluctantly did, while Molly dressed and complained about her hair and wondered aloud what they were going to do now. They certainly couldn't leave Cull and his henchmen here for a nurse or doctor to find, and they couldn't take them with them, and they couldn't kill them, and they couldn't hide them and they—

"Molly," Lincoln said wearily, "stand at the door and keep watch."

"What are you going to do?"

He glared, she moved, and he gestured with the gun at the two men. They balked. He suggested with the barrel that their lady friends wouldn't appreciate their impending condition if they refused much longer. They considered the implications. He gestured again, impatiently, and after exchanging defeated glances they squeezed themselves into the closet, Takana warning Molahu to keep his Polynesian hands to himself. Lincoln closed and locked the door, tested it to be sure, and whirled just as Cull flung himself up from the floor. Not wanting to fire the weapon restrained him somewhat, and they ended up grappling across the room, slamming into the bed, the wall, and finally coming up against the windowsill.

Molly, alarmed, danced around them anxiously, attempting to find some way to scream in Cull's ear again without alerting the medical staff in the hallway.

Linc, the back of his skull pressed against the pane, his arms pinned at his sides, finally managed to bring his knee up. Cull anticipated the move and shifted to one side, just enough to allow Linc to wrench one of his arms free, reach up as high as he could, and clamp his fingers around the man's throat.

Cull's eyes widened as his air supply was strangled.

Linc's eyes widened when he saw Molly lifting the chair over her head.

Cull brought his own knee up, and Linc deflected its trajectory with a thigh.

Molly brought the chair down across Cull's back.

The door to the closet began splintering.

Cull stiffened, groaned, and sagged to the floor, and Linc leapt over his body, grabbed Molly's arm and raced out of the room. There was a nurse at the station in the hall's center, but she was busily watching the Intensive Care monitors and did not see them slip into the emergency stairwell.

"Now what?" Molly said as they raced down the concrete steps toward the ground floor.

"Now we find a way to get to the airport."

"Why?"

"Hawaii," he said, coming up against the fire door and slamming down on the handle.

They walked hurriedly along a well-lit, deserted corridor until they found themselves in the main lobby. There were a dozen or more people milling about the reception counter paying no attention to anyone but themselves. Arm in arm, then, they strolled through the entrance and looked helplessly at the almost deserted parking lot. There were no taxis, and they had no time to call one; there were no buses, no vans, and at the moment no visitors arriving or leaving. It wasn't until Linc stepped off the curb and was nearly run down by a sleek plastic Corvette that he knew they were saved.

The automobile stopped with an apologetic squeal of its brakes, and backed up, the driver looking anxiously over his shoulder to be sure he hadn't harmed anyone.

Linc pulled open the passenger door and shoved Molly inside. Then he squeezed mightily in beside her and grinned.

"Officer Oberon," he said, "can you give us a lift?"

Oberon, now in striking civilian clothes that seemed ripped directly off the back of an escaped lounge lizard, gaped.

Molly, batting her eyelashes furiously, leaned close to him and smiled.

Linc, who saw Takana and Molahu bulling their way through the crowded lobby, suggested that they might miss their flight, and all would be revealed if only the off-duty security guard would move in the opposite direction.

Oberon, too stunned by Molly's proximity and his remarkably unpleasant luck, obeyed mindlessly, and they were soon barreling toward the airport on the freeway.

Despite the cramped quarters, Lincoln managed to keep an eye on the back window, searching for Cull's men, or perhaps Cull himself, while Molly rattled on about her student days at UCLA, Stanford, and the University of Nebraska. Oberon didn't once ask her why she'd attended so many schools— he was too busy trying to figure out how he was going to explain this to his ex-wives and his current, volatile, girlfriend.

Then Lincoln saw a car weaving through the traffic toward them. He suggested a greater speed. Oberon suggested a method of lightening the load. The pursuing automobile pulled up behind them and rode the bumper.

"Lincoln," Molly said when she noticed.

"Yeah, I know."

"Know what?" Oberon asked fearfully, thinking of the salad and the electrified metal detector.

There was no time for an answer.

The back window shattered at an explosion, and when Molly screamed, Lincoln saw Officer Oberon slump over the wheel—in the lefthand lane, doing eighty-three miles per hour and his foot jammed on the accelerator.

ELEVEN

AT LINC'S ORDER, AND TOO TERRIFIED TO PROTEST the insanity of it all, Molly reached clumsily across the unconscious Oberon and did her best to grab the wheel. The Corvette swerved from lane to lane sharply as she sought a straight line from the awkward angle of her perception. Another volley of gunshots perforated the backs of the seats. Linc squeezed himself as best he could toward the lefthand well and yanked at Oberon's leg. It was stiff. He punched at it, snarled at it, punched again and finally managed to slide the foot away from the accelerator. Then, paying no attention to Molly's yelping protests, and trying not to pay attention to the sickening sway and lurch of the car, he leaned back, stretched out his own foot and aimed for the brake pedal.

He missed.

He aimed again, and missed again.

The angle was wrong, Oberon's legs were too tangled, and Molly kept bleating about becoming a statistic.

A truck loomed ahead of them, its running lights

amber and red, its wheels almost as large as the Corvette itself.

Linc wondered why the hell the car was still going so fast, and when he looked down saw that the foot was indeed away, but the toes were not. With a groan he tried a third time, then cursed and opened his door, held onto the handle and leaned out slightly. The wind tore through his hair and nearly blinded him; the sounds of freeway traffic finally catching on and getting out of the way made him grimace in anticipation of a collision; but by keeping his grip on the handle and holding onto the car's frame over the door he was able, after kicking at Oberon's legs again, to stretch out his own foot and jab at the brake, a second time, and a third before he connected.

The Corvette belched smoke from its undercarriage, filling his eyes with a harsh stinging and his nostrils with an acrid stench that made him gag.

The truck moved over into the middle lane.

So did the Corvette.

He stabbed at the brake again, swearing at the top of his voice when his foot kept slipping off.

Molly aimed precariously for the left lane and instead reached the narrow shoulder, scraping the car's side with a metallic shriek before rebounding and nearly fishtailing.

A shot webbed the glass of the passenger door over Linc's head, and another came within a hand's breadth of shattering his elbow.

The brake again, and it seemed to him they were finally slowing down. The rest of the nighttime traffic was not, however, and it blew past him, shaking him, making him realize that even if he wanted to, he would be unable to get back into the car.

He was stuck, about four inches above the road's surface, and his hands were slipping from both frame and handle.

He yelled wordlessly over the roar of the wind, and attempted to regrip the frame. Perspiration made his fingers slick, and tension made them increasingly weaker. His rump began to slide off the seat, and he could feel without imagining it the rush of the road under his hip pocket.

The car shifted right again, into the next lane, definitely slower but not slow enough.

He aimed another lunge at the brake. As he did, successfully, his left hand came away from the car and he flailed wildly before swinging it over to grab onto the top of the door. Now he was facing downward, watching the reflecting lights buried in the dividing lines wink past him in a blur.

His right hand slipped away from the handle, and he swung again, grabbing onto the frame alongside his seat. Now he was chest down to the road, and when he looked behind he saw the black car closing in on him, on the inside lane.

Sonofabitch is going too fast, he thought.

It closed, and he could see the silhouettes of the two men in the front seat. Neither was reaching out a window with a gun; they were going to be content to clip him in half.

His left hand began slipping.

His right hand cramped.

A pebble kicked up from the road and took a small piece of his left cheek.

The other car was close enough now so that the headlamps blinded him, and he turned away, into the wind, and decided it wouldn't hurt to think of a short, powerful prayer about now.

Then the Corvette suddenly lurched, bucked, slowed considerably and swayed into the righthand lane ahead of the black car. The shoulder, then, and when he chanced a look up he saw that the verge was bordered by a hill. A very close hill that was going to give him a haircut if Molly didn't do something soon.

Another bucking, more lurching, and just as his left hand gave way, with nothing else to cling to, the Corvette came to a shuddering, backfiring stop.

"Damn," Molly said, "I hate standard transmissions."

He lay on his back on the slick grassy hillside, arms akimbo, his eyes closed and his ears paying no heed to the noise of passing traffic. In an odd way, he was hoping he was dead. Molly sat beside him, legs up and chin on her knees, one hand plucking at the grass and scattering the blades to the wind. Once in a while, her teeth began chattering. Every so often she would break into a violent trembling and hug her shins until she stopped; every so often he felt his arms falling off and would wiggle his fingers to be sure he still had his hands.

The Corvette sat on the shoulder, Oberon slumped behind the wheel.

"Well," she said at last, her voice high and weak, "at least my hair is straight now."

"Wonderful."

She let her gaze follow the traffic's flow, side to side as if watching a tennis match that bored her silly.

"Those men—"

"They won't be back. They figure if I'm not dead, I'm at least too battered to do much damage."

"Wow, how do you know that?"

"They're stupid."

"And how do you know that?"

"They work for Florenz Cull."

"I see."

An ambulance wailed past them, and she pulled away from it, wincing. "We can't stay here long, y'know. A cop's going to be by pretty soon and want to know what we're doing here, in the middle of the night."

"Where was he before, when we needed him?"

She shrugged, and watched the lights of the warehouses and homes across the freeway.

"I don't think," he said, "we're far from the airport."

"How can you tell?"

"I can smell the fuel they use."

"Oh."

He pushed himself up, grunting, to a sitting position. "It's a talent we acrophobes develop."

"Oh."

He rubbed his face hard with his palms, brushed back his hair, and took a deep breath. Coughed. Wrinkled his nose at the layer of August smog that hung over the valley, and tried to remember what breathing was like back in Maine.

"What," she said, "are we going to do about Officer Oberon?"

"Is he dead?"

She swallowed before nodding.

"Damn."

She looked at him sideways. "Do people always die when they meet up with you? I mean, do you always cause this much trouble?"

Slipping a little on the grass, he rose and stretched, took her arm and brought her to her feet. After a perfunctory dusting of their clothes, he led her to the car, peered in and confirmed the man's condition—there were three small bullet holes along the length of his spine.

"No," he said as he closed the door. "Not always."

"But sometimes."

With a hitch of his belt, he headed toward the exit ramp a hundred yards distant. "I remind you, Miss Partridge, that bringing me into this was your idea, not mine. I am a tailor by profession, and only occasionally an idiot who does things for people who won't let him alone until he does it."

Tagging along beside him, at times nearly skipping to keep up, she frowned. "I didn't mean it that way."

"I know. I'm sorry."

"But you are a lot of trouble."

Rather than shove her in front of the nearest automobile, he walked on, leading her silently off the ramp and onto a broad thoroughfare lined with dead cars at the curbs and seedy, darkened shops. In the near distance, southward, he saw a gaudy billboard advertising a cut-rate, splendid, no-frills but all the necessities tour of the entire Hawaiian Island chain, though certain restrictions applied and not all planes were available for this incredible offer.

"A sign," he said in a tone of mock revelation.

"I can see it," she told him grumpily. "And I can read, too."

He sighed without a sound and walked on. It didn't take him long to realize, somewhat gloomily, that they were the only two human beings within sight who were moving on their feet, perhaps the only two in the entire city, and most certainly in this particular neighborhood which, as they left the first hour behind them, changed into one filled with low office buildings with spotlighted fountains, motels with spotlighted palm trees, and the occasional service station and twenty-four-hour food market spotlighted with signs large enough to be seen in Arizona. The noise of arriving and departing aircraft increased, the aftermath of the overhead roaring creating a deeper silence than he would have liked. Even the infrequent automobiles seemed to have muffled their engines and their tires and the music that should have been blaring from their open windows.

A neon sign buzzed at them as they passed beneath it.

The street shimmered as if coated with water and oil.

Midway through their second hour she took his hand, less a token of affection than a quest for security.

At the next service station they waited in the

shadows until a series of cars was lined up at the pumps and a handful of people milled about, asking directions and arguing over prices; then they used the none-too-sanitary rest rooms to clean themselves up, examine their bruises, and surrender to the unavoidable fact that a week at a health spa would still leave their essential humanity in serious question.

"Mr. Blackthorne," she said as they moved on, signs to LAX finally in abundance, "this isn't fun."

"You could say that."

"I mean, there is a certain amount of logic in continuing this madness since it's frowned upon to leave important work undone in this society, especially when it deals with matters of cataclysm and lost culture. But it isn't fun anymore."

"It was before?"

"A little. Maine is nice, the moose were nice—"

"Moose?"

"Sure."

"What moose?"

"The ones I saw after that truck nearly ran us down in that picnic area. Three or four of them, I think. I didn't really stop to get a close look."

"Three or four," he said flatly.

"Sure. And rowing on the river was nice, too. Kind of romantic, in a way."

He refused to nod or shake his head. Any movement now other than simply walking was, he was positive, going to cause his arms to fall from his shoulders, and his legs to crumble from his aching hips. A reaction to his recent experience, and the strain his muscles took, though understanding that didn't make any of it any more bearable.

Then, suddenly, he stopped on a corner, took her gently by the shoulders and smiled. "Molly," he said, "Oberon bothers you."

"Yes." She would not meet his gaze. "We . . . we just left him there."

"Yes, we did. If we had waited for a policeman, we would have had to answer a lot of questions, the answers to which no one would understand. Not to mention the fact that Molahu and Takana were not around to share the blame."

"I understand that," she insisted softly, "but—"

"It isn't going to get any better, not with Florenz Cull after our hides, and your brother's."

"I guess."

"And if you want to forget it and go on home, wherever that is, it's all right."

She seemed to consider it as she pushed her hair away from her eyes. "What about you?"

"Not now. Before, it was ridiculous. Now it's personal. Besides," he said, grinning, "if you don't want to save the world, I'm going to have to."

She was slow in smiling, but when it finally came he was relieved, and with arms about each other's waists they crossed the wide street and headed cautiously for the terminal. Just shy of the entrance they crossed over into the vast parking lot and waited for nearly an hour behind a charitably described junk heap that had taken up two spaces in order to preserve its rustic finish. They watched the pedestrian traffic for signs of Cull and his men or any inquisitive police; they discussed the relative merits of the airlines they should take to the Islands, Lincoln making a strong but futile case for an ocean liner out of Long Beach; and Molly did her best, with comb and spit, to make them both look presentable.

Finally, he decided they would either have to pay a fee or make their move. With a touch to Molly's arm, then, they walked as fast as they could without running into the brightly lit ticket area.

"And another thing," he said before they reached the counter.

"What?"

"Being on that river was not romantic."

"Good god, don't you like water, either?"

"You could drown in it, don't you know that? The stuff gets into your lungs and inhibits the breathing apparatus from functioning properly and good god, I'm starting to sound like you."

"I think," she muttered sourly, "I've made a mistake."

"Indeed you have," said Florenz Cull from behind them.

Lincoln whirled, but could do nothing about the way the tall man hugged him as though they were old friends meeting at the airport; nor could he do anything about the stabbing he felt in his side.

It burned.

It spread rapidly to his arms and legs and paralyzed them.

Then it spread to his eyes, and Cull's white hair turned slowly black.

TWELVE

IT WAS, WITHOUT A DOUBT, THE MOST IMPRESSIVE beast he had ever seen, and certainly worth the wait after all the trouble he had gone through to find one —a bull moose that looked nothing like Teddy Roosevelt, with an antler spread that almost forbade it travel in the forest, with a bulk that made the ground tremble as it walked in its own stately procession, and with one unwinking white eye that stared mercilessly at him as it rode him across the undulating plain. He had no idea what he was doing riding a moose, and the faster the beast moved the more uneasy he became. It was one thing to observe these creatures in their natural habitat; it was quite another to hitch a ride on one, especially when it was wearing a flowered shirt and a lei about its neck.

Then it tripped in some unseen depression, and though its eye never wavered he felt himself beginning to fall. His stomach crept rapidly toward his throat, and his brain decided to expand through the gaps left by the hair that had deserted his scalp. He flailed for balance, moaning loudly that he didn't want to die under the rampaging hooves of a maddened denizen of a black forest, and suddenly, with a strength he didn't know he had, he thrust himself erect.

The moose vanished.

The eye sped skyward until it transformed itself into the moon.

And Molly looked at him quizzically. "Have you," she said, "ever thought about seeing somebody for this fascination you have with mooses?"

"Moose," he corrected. "And how the hell did you get here?"

"I was carried," she said sourly. "They didn't think I could walk on my own."

"They?"

"For god's sake, Lincoln, wake up, will you? We're in trouble. Serious trouble."

He accepted a damp cloth she pressed into his hand and used it to wipe his face, the back of his neck, and did his best to clear his eyes. When he thought he could see and think straight, he looked around and found himself in an airliner's seat, a very wide, leather one, in a cabin that held only a dozen of them. Some were placed around tables bolted to the deck; others were by themselves as though to signal privacy. The walls were papered in soft dawn colors, and when he looked behind him toward the rear of the craft, he could see a silver Chinese screen separating this area from another behind. The deck was carpeted in a deep wine, and when he looked up he could see a series of small perforations which, he supposed, were part of a fire extinguishing system.

Ahead, past the galley, he could see the door to

the cockpit, and in front of it, Eddie Takana sitting in a chair with his arms folded over his chest and his eyes tightly closed. In his lap was a crossbow.

"Well, I'll be double-damned," he said with something akin to disgusted admiration. "We've been kidnapped."

Molly rolled her eyes and dropped back in her seat.

"Lincoln," he said then.

"That's right," she said, looking a bit worried now. "That's your name."

"No, no. I mean, you called me Lincoln before instead of Mr. Blackthorne." He stretched, realizing he wasn't tied or chained or nailed to his seat. The mild turbulence that had awakened him had passed, and when he looked out the window and down, all he could see was the moon reflected in an avenue of silver across rolling waves.

"Don't let it go to your head," she told him. "I did it in the heat of the moment."

"We're over the ocean," he announced, snapping away from the window. "There are waves and things down there."

"That's right."

He frowned, shook his head to scatter the last effects of the drug he'd been administered, and sighed. "We're on our way to Hawaii."

"Right again."

"And I suppose," he said, jerking a thumb over his shoulder, "that Cull and the other Don Ho are behind that screen."

"Nope."

"What?"

"As far as I can tell, Eddie is our only guard, unless you count the pilot and the co-pilot."

He leaned forward, staring at the sleeping man. "I don't get it. What's the catch?"

"The catch is, Eddie is very good with that thing, and even if we do manage to overpower him, that door there is double-locked and the two guys up front are probably armed to the teeth. And even if we should have the skills to get past Eddie, the door, and the two guys up front, there's no way we'll survive afterward because the plane will crash in the middle of the Pacific Ocean and we'll drown, or get eaten by sharks.

"Unless," she said hopefully, "you know how to fly one of these things."

He gave her a look; she slumped lower in her seat.

"Lincoln, if I don't make it," she whispered, "I want you to carry on for me."

"If you don't make it," he said, "there's not much chance I will, either."

"Oh. Yeah."

"It's really quite diabolical," he said. "But why didn't Cull and his other thug come with us? Surely this is better than flying a commercial airliner, assuming there are better grades of flying."

"How should I know? I've been kidnapped too, remember? I'm just along for the ride, like you are. And if we don't do something soon we're going to be trapped forever in Cull's hideout and I won't be able to get hold of my brother, who is no doubt having a great time down there scaring the hell out of the tourists."

Lincoln sympathized with her concern, but even more, he realized that she, and Cull, believed that Partridge's use of this statuette had resulted in the recent eruptions of Kilauea, one of the most impressive, and potentially destructive, volcanoes in the chain.

Yet, if he recalled his geography correctly, there were no large cities near the lava flow, or government installations, or army or navy bases. So what was the point? For those who knew what the Soldier could do, whatever that was, the display only served as a beacon for their greed. For everyone else, it provided a startling show on the evening news.

It made about as much real sense as Cull not traveling on his own airplane with them.

He looked out at the star-pocked night sky again, at the ocean below, and realized that to see the water as clearly as he did they would have to be cruising far below the regular air lanes. Another oddity, since the only purpose for that would be to keep the plane from showing up on pesky radar screens. And Cull wouldn't give a damn about that since the aircraft was certainly large enough to have been seen in its take-off. Unless, of course, being seen in its take-off was part of the plan, the other part being not to be seen in its landing because it wouldn't be landing at all—at least not where it was supposed to. Which, he thought, was distressing since it couldn't fly forever, either.

"Damn," he said.

Molly looked at him, alarmed. "The moose again?"

He quieted her with a brusque gesture and stared at Takana, who had shifted somewhat, his hands drifting lovingly down over the metal crossbow which had more balance weights on it than a twenty-foot clock.

"Oh . . . damn."

"Lincoln, what *is* it?"

He patted her leg paternally. "Tell me something —did you see the pilot and co-pilot go to the flight deck? You said they were there, but did you actually see them? Or have you seen Eddie talking to them?"

"Well, no, not exactly. After Cull doped you, he showed me that cane of his, the one with the funny tiger head? He said he would do wonders to my face if I screamed, and I believed him. I think he's crazy, if you want to know what I think."

"For once, I think you're right."

She looked at him, frowned, looked away, looked back, and decided to pass. "So then they—Cull and Eddie—carried you along between them like you were drunk or something, and Loop took me and we went out of the terminal to this plane on the runway. I tried to look desperate, like I was being kidnapped, but no one paid any attention to me. I think it was Cull. He was so tall they were too busy looking at him instead of at me. That," she added glumly, "is not very flattering."

"I'm sorry."

"It's all right. It's not your fault."

"The plane," he prompted. "What happened then?"

"Well, then Loop carried me in, Eddie strapped me down, and by the time you were dumped into the seat too, we were already ready to go. It was unnerving, Lincoln, and I intend to kill Cull very slowly for his treatment of me. After all, there have to be some sort of standards, even in situations like this, don't you agree? I mean—oh my god."

Lincoln agreed.

He suspected that shortly after the plane had left coastal waters, the pilot who had overseen the take-off had taken off, leaving Eddie behind to maintain the fiction that they were heading straight for Hawaii, no stops along the way, and once there Cull would have other plans for them.

Eddie, however, was a decoy.

No doubt, he thought with narrowed eyes, the man had his own orders, among which was a disappearing act of his own when they had reached a prearranged spot, probably just past midway to their supposed destination. He also suspected that there wasn't enough fuel on board to get them anywhere at all.

What they were riding in, then, was one hell of an elaborate and expensive hearse.

Thirty minutes later the plane swung slightly to the west, and Lincoln could not be sure that it didn't also lose a few hundred feet of altitude in the turning. Molly took hold of his arm, gripping it tightly, and when he followed the direction of her gaze he realized that the trip was almost over.

Takana, moving rather lightly for a man of his bulk, rose from his seat and smiled at them. Then he reached under his seat and pulled out a long and unpleasant-looking quarrel, which he loaded swiftly and expertly into the crossbow.

"Are you going to kill us?" Molly asked timorously.

Eddie's smile broadened to a grin. "No, Miss, not if you stay where you are," he said, his voice the sweetest and most surprising soprano Lincoln had ever heard outside the last performance of the Vienna Boys Choir. "But you don't move now, you hear? You stay right there."

"Oh sure," she said, nodding agreeably. "Of course. Whatever you say."

Takana vanished into the galley, and just as Lincoln had measured the distance between his seat and the galley doorway, thinking he might be able to propel himself across the twenty or so feet of open space in time to catch the Japanese-Hawaiian off his guard, the man returned, his bulk considerably increased by a parachute strapped to his back.

"Oh no," Molly whispered, and tightened her grip on Lincoln's arm. "Oh no, it's not fair."

There was a table just this side of the galley wall, and he placed the crossbow on it, adjusted the straps around his chest and between his legs, and frowned in disappointed anger when Lincoln shook off Molly's hand and rose.

"You are not to move," the man said, whipping up the crossbow to aim it at Linc's chest.

"I ought to be able to stretch a little," he said, putting action to words.

"You'd better sit, round eyes, or when I open the door you'll get sucked out of here like spaghetti off a plate."

Molly gasped at the analogy and hastened to fasten her seatbelt; Linc, on the other hand, knew the man needed two hands to crank open the door. He smiled, smoothed his shirt into his jeans, did a few deep knee bends, and strode back toward the Chinese screen.

"Stay where you are," Takana ordered.

Lincoln stopped short of the decoration and looked over his shoulder. "Shoot if you must this old gray head," he said, "but I have to use the john."

"There's no time," Takana told him, and clenched his teeth suddenly.

"Ah, so I was right."

"Lincoln, please," Molly said. "Do what he tells you."

Takana brought the crossbow stock to his shoulder.

Lincoln moved to the side of the screen and looked around it. There was, perhaps, fifteen feet of empty flooring between it and the rear bulkhead, and the door to the restroom on the left. He could see nothing he could use as a weapon.

"Blackthorne!" Takana called.

Lincoln shrugged, and ducked around the screen.

"Damnit!" he heard the man say.

"Lincoln, for god's sake!"

He knelt quickly at the base of the screen, thinking that the man would either rush back and try to aerate him with the quarrel, or force him back into his seat, or leave the aircraft without bothering to do anything. But Takana had to make up his mind quickly, because the plane banked gently again, and if there was a boat below waiting to pick him up, he couldn't afford to lose any time.

Lincoln inched back until his left foot was braced for launching against the wall. He took several deep breaths. He tried to make himself as small as possible, hoping the deadly quarrel would be off the mark if it were released. And he reached to his left in case he had to grab onto something when the door was opened and Takana left.

He thought he had covered everything.

Then Molly screamed, and he grabbed onto the rest room door frame, gritting his teeth and waiting for the air pressure to drop in the cabin, the resulting temporary vacuum sucking him to his death.

It didn't happen.

He heard a door slam all right, but there was no loss of pressure, no rush of air, no sudden influx of numbing cold.

"Damnit, Lincoln," Molly shouted, "are you going to stay in there all day?"

He waited another few seconds before standing, another five before coming around the screen in time to see her rushing toward the cockpit door. She grabbed the handle and pulled, kicked, pulled, and turned to lean against it.

"He's gone," she said.

"That way?"

"Of course. How else did the pilot get out without our knowing it?"

"I'll be damned."

Then the aircraft lurched, and he stumbled forward, barely stopping himself before he reached her.

"Lincoln," she said, "I can't fly."

"Neither can the plane."

"We're going to die!"

"I think so," he agreed, "but not from a crash."

And he pointed to the holes he had seen in the ceiling, and the puffs of white gas that hissed into the cabin.

THIRTEEN

LINC ORDERED MOLLY TO GET AS LOW ON THE FLOOR as she could and cover her mouth; then he dashed into the small, elaborate galley. He knew that Cull, while probably not enamored of federal regulations, would have as much safety equipment on board the private plane as he felt necessary. Now, if he could only find some of it, they just might have a chance to get out of this mess alive.

The hissing of the gas jets grew louder.

He thought he could smell the faint scent of almonds.

Time, he told himself as he slammed open cupboard doors; I've got to have some time!

Molly called to him, pleading with him to get down, but he couldn't stop now. Somewhere in this galley was something he could use to—

"Ah ha!" he shouted.

"I'm not hungry!" she called back.

There, in a small compartment beside the compact refrigeration unit, was a pair of fire extinguishers. He tugged them out to the counter, grunting at their weight; then he grabbed a towel, soaked it and tied it around his face. When he was sure it wouldn't slip, he darted back into the cabin, took a deep breath, and swung the butt of the extinguisher against the window. His arms stung, yet he didn't drop the cylinder, only swung it around again, and a third time, and a fourth that produced a series of cracks in the pressure-tested glass. A fifth widened them, and a sixth shattered them completely.

Though they were low enough not to cause a severe drop in air pressure, the resulting suction, combined with a wind that coursed through the cabin, began sucking the gas out. He staggered against the galley's outside wall and grinned to himself, pleased, and relieved.

And slapped his forehead and groaned when he saw that the flow of gas had increased, and it wasn't leaving the cabin rapidly enough.

They were still going to die, with a million square miles of fresh air rushing past them.

Well, hell, he thought, and looked up, examining the ceiling until he located the slots where the emergency oxygen masks would drop.

The fast-pouring gas whirled now in the wind that tore at his clothes, his hair, and made it seem as if he were struggling through a supernatural fog. His eyes began to tear, and he could feel a raw burning begin in his throat.

Molly whimpered something behind him, but he could not understand her—the cabin was beginning to spin slowly on an invisible axis, and as he reached up to touch the oxygen compartment outline, his arms felt as if they had been sheathed in cool lead.

He leaned over for a moment to gather his

strength, then suddenly reared and pounded on the ceiling with the butt of the extinguisher, watching all the time as the cabin continued to fill with a drifting white mist. His lungs found it difficult to draw air through the moist towel; his arms grew more weary and the extinguisher more weighted; and a glance over his shoulder told him Molly had slipped into the galley, probably believing she might find safety there, more so than at the cockpit door.

A shame, he thought, as he swung the extinguisher around again, and then yelled when the release mechanism gave and four yellow masks dropped into the cabin.

He grabbed one and yanked on the clear plastic umbilical cord, then slapped the plastic over his mouth and nose and took a deep breath.

The mist thickened.

It was, he thought, only a stopgap measure—he could hardly stand here until the plane finally ditched into the Pacific.

But at the moment it added precious seconds to his life, and gave him the opportunity to think of something else.

Then Molly grabbed his shoulder and tried to pull him away.

Delirious, he thought; the gas has made the poor kid delirious—the first sign of the end.

She refused him, however, when he tried to press a mask into her hands, and he was ready to force it on her, to save her life in spite of herself, when she cupped his face in her palms and yanked his head around.

And pointed at the open cockpit door.

He gaped for only a second before tossing aside the mask and following her through, slamming the door behind them and dropping into the pilot's seat. She took the co-pilot's, and they slapped on the heavy masks that, at the flick of a red switch, filled their lungs with fresh air.

He leaned back and closed his eyes.

Molly's humming was muffled.

Then he swallowed a trace of bile and looked toward her, pointed at the on-board radio nestled against her throat, and waited until she had activated it.

"How the hell did you do that?" he asked.

She held up a knife she'd taken from the galley. "It's easy when you know how. All oppressed minorities learn a few illegal things now and then."

He remembered the burglar's tools in her knapsack and was not surprised. Then he looked front, and saw the stars, the night, and the ocean below them.

"Oh, brother," he said.

"I think," she whispered, "maybe it would be better if we just opened the door."

He stared at the incredible conglomeration of instrumentation in front of him, reached tentatively for the steering grip, and yanked his hands back when the column shifted on its own and the plane backed gently to the west.

Suddenly, he grinned.

"What?" she said. "You see an angel?"

"I have, and he has one eye."

"You're kidding."

He pointed to the column. "It moved."

"Well, of course it did. It's on auto-pilot, and it's going to dump us in the water!"

He watched for a long moment, not wanting to give himself hope until he was sure. Then he shrugged. Hell, with all those gizmos and needles and lights and dots, he wouldn't be sure even if he had the manual on his lap and John Wayne whistling "The High and the Mighty" in his ear.

"We're not going to crash," he said.

"What?"

"Of course not."

She reached over to put a hand against his forehead. "It was the gas, right? You're not thinking straight. You got a small dose of it, and now you're hallucinating."

"No I'm not," he said, laughing and liking the sound of it. "No, I'm not."

"Lincoln—"

"No," he said, capturing her hand and holding it in both of his. "Think about it for a minute."

She did, and shook her head helplessly.

"Consider, then," he told her. "This is Cull's own private plane, right? He dumps us on it, takes off, and then deserts us in the middle of the Pacific Ocean." He took a second to shudder at all that air out there, and all that water down there. Molly was right—this wasn't fun at all. "Naturally, we assume we're going to crash. The plane will go down, so will we, and there'll be no evidence of anything. We'll just vanish into Judge Crater heaven."

"Right," she said. "So why are you so happy?"

"I have a question for you."

She looked doubtfully out the windscreen. "Go ahead."

"Why did he try to gas us?"

"To kill us, stupid."

"But we were going to crash!"

She frowned. "He wanted to make sure we didn't survive."

He pointed to the ocean. "Out there?"

"Maybe he respects your abilities."

"That's probably true," he said shamelessly, "but you're missing the point. Cull never intended this plane to crash. We were supposed to die on board, the plane would land, and our bodies would be taken off."

She stared at the instrument panel, at the Pacific, at him. "Magic?"

"Electronics," he said. "A sophisticated drone."

"Oh! Remote control."

He shrugged. "Not quite. More like pre-programming an on-board computer guidance system."

The aircraft made an adjustment, and he decided he didn't like seeing the steering mechanisms move on their own like that—it smacked too much of an intelligence greater than his.

An hour passed, and he was forced to admit that watching the stars as they were, without being washed out by city lights, was an absorbing and almost hypnotic experience; the moon caught flecks of phosphorescence on the surface below, and made it seem less like water than a rolling dark plain half magic, half demonic.

"Lincoln?"

He turned to her, smiling.

"If what you said before is true, why did the pilot and Takana bail out?"

He opened his mouth to answer, and closed it again when he realized he didn't know. To have them picked up at sea made sense, but it also added a number of unnecessary complications to the operation. What Cull should have done was provide them with gas masks, and a means to pump the poison out of the plane once the deed was done. The arrangements would have been ridiculously simple, and it would have provided a back-up system in case the gas didn't work as it should have.

In fact, the more he thought about it, the less this whole episode made sense. Why the hell didn't Cull just have Takana shoot them and be done with it?

He took a closer look around the cockpit then, and realized with a silent groan that unless both the pilot and Eddie Takana were able to transform themselves instantly into skydiving midgets with matching parachutes, there was no possible exit to the outside from here.

Oh, damn, he thought.

"Bless you," Molly said then, taking off her mask.

"Huh?"

"You sneezed. I said bless you."

He took off his mask as well, and frowned. "But I didn't sneeze."

"Sure you did. I heard you."

He turned to argue, and something caught his attention behind him. He looked down at the deck and saw a large handle that had been flush with the deck when they'd entered, and was now upright and rotating.

"Well," he said, working feverishly on his straps.

"Well what?"

"Well, I'll be damned."

He eased out of the pilot's seat and knelt on the floor, seeing now the outline of a hatch, watching as the handle rotated a few times more, then was pulled down until it lay within its depression. A quick search found the hinges, and he knelt behind them, waiting as the hatch cover vibrated slightly before slowly beginning to rise.

Molly, unbuckled but unable to join him because of the confines of the cabin, watched fearfully.

The cover rose.

The plane banked right.

Lincoln shifted back awkwardly to permit the cover to tilt in his direction. Once it settled back, there was a moment when nothing moved. Then he rose abruptly and swooped forward to grab the shoulders of the man who was scrambling out of the compartment below. The man popped out of the opening with a squeal and was flung sideways, landing against the door with a hollow thud that seemed to rattle the cabin. Lincoln was on him instantly, pinning him to the floor with his knees, one fist raised to perform minor cosmetic surgery on his nose when, suddenly, he froze.

"Well, for crying out loud," he said.

"What?" Molly said.

He looked down at the man and shook his head. "I don't suppose you'd care to explain."

Arturo Pigmeo, his initial shock at the accosting passing when he recognized Lincoln's voice, grinned. "Lordy, it's you, you old air pirate! What fortune!"

"Who is it?" Molly asked.

Lincoln backed off Pigmeo and brushed at his jeans while the tiny man struggled to regain his feet. Once he had, and was sitting in the navigator's chair, he beamed.

"I thought I was going to die down there, Lincoln. You don't know what it's like to be in the dark."

Lincoln stood over him, hands loose on his hips in case they required a flurry of exercise, and he said nothing, just listened to the man babbling until at last, Pigmeo quieted. Then he pointed behind him. "What," he said, "were you doing down there? You're supposed to be in Pittsburgh."

Molly whispered something to him, but he waved her silent.

"I was in the Pittsburgh," Pigmeo protested. "But now I am here."

"Why?"

"Because," said Salome from behind him, "he wants to see you die."

FOURTEEN

LINCOLN AND MOLLY SAT SILENTLY ON THE RIGHT side of the cabin, each strapped into a leather seat and facing a narrow teak table whose highly polished surface was graciously indented for holding glasses and plates and the occasional hand of gin rummy against the vagaries of air currents. On the other side of the table, facing them, Arturo was brushing his curly hair thoughtfully while Salome, with a moue of distaste for a deed that had to be done, tackled the dust his tuxedo had accumulated in the compartment below the cockpit.

Takana, after hastily stuffing the broken window with several blankets and a broad webbing of tape, was forward in the galley, humming an interminable medley of Don Ho's greatest hits and fixing a snack.

The pilot, whom Lincoln still hadn't seen, was snoring in a pull-down bed behind the Chinese screen.

The private plane droned on.

It had taken some while for Lincoln to sort matters out to his satisfaction, and when he had he managed to keep his growing dismay to himself.

Arturo had indeed been in suburban Pittsburgh at Cull's stern request, and the negotiations they went through were obvious by the fading, well-placed bruises that pocked the little man's cheeks. Since Pigmeo was nothing if not a practical man in terms of his survival route along the evolutionary scale, he understood perfectly Cull's point of view— either stop being a nuisance and join the cause, or spend the rest of eternity singing in a celestial opera where the fat lady never dies and the spear carriers aren't joking.

"It is a matter of priorities," Pigmeo said with a sorrowful shake of his head. "One must reevaluate now and then so that one does not stagnate and grow careless, don't you agree?"

Lincoln did, and told him that he held no grudge. Whether the energetic if not dynamic duo had shown up or not, he was still faced with the same problem—what to do when they landed in Hawaii and Cull, faced with the disappointment of them not expiring as they should have, lost his temper. He had seen that display once before, and had seen the victims of the tall man's wrath; Pigmeo's lumps were mere mosquito bites by comparison.

"When do we land?" he asked.

"Two hours, give or take," Pigmeo said with a check of his gold watch. "Shortly after dawn."

Lincoln yawned, long and loud and without apology, and saw Salome blink furiously to hold back one of her own. It must have been terribly uncomfortable for her down there, he thought; and she was evidently not pleased, especially after having to scramble out the rear of the hotel in Maine just before it blew up and seared the back of that seductive green dress. She really ought to get some rest or she wasn't going to be much good to anyone once they touched down. When he suggested it, however, in the kindest possible manner, she sneered in his general direction and proceeded to work on her coif.

A look to Molly, and he smiled—despite it all, she was dozing.

Takana came out of the galley with a heaping tray of cocktail sandwiches he placed on the table. Lincoln squinted at the garish shirt until the man filled his own hands and walked off; then he took one himself, holding it until the others had made their selections and were already eating before he took his first bite. A brief period of waiting to be sure he wasn't going to be drugged, poisoned, or otherwise exotically incapacitated, and he had several more, thinking that Takana's skills amazingly weren't limited to the production of general mayhem and all-purpose disposal; the only problem was, the guy had a thing about passion fruit and tuna fish.

After finishing, he leaned back and closed his eyes without saying a word. He still hadn't figured out the purpose behind this elaborate show of technological wizardry, and was determined to do so before they landed; it might, after all, have some bearing on his future.

He fell asleep.

He awoke when the cabin flooded with sunlight.

Cautiously he opened his eyes, noting that Arturo was still in the same seat and snoring, Salome had stretched out across two others just by the galley, and Takana and the pilot were nowhere in sight. It would have been the perfect time for a magnificent, if somewhat gaudy and reckless, show of heroics, except for the fact that he had no weapon other than the small knife sheathed on his wrist, he couldn't fly the plane, and he hadn't the faintest idea what he was going to do once he touched ground.

So he closed his eyes again, and didn't wake up until he felt the plane shudder violently.

"Nuts," he whispered, and refused to look out the window where the Islands were rushing up to meet the belly of the plane. He hoped the pilot—computer or human—knew the difference between land and sea, because there wasn't much of the former and rather too much of the latter out there. One miss, and they would be rowing this damned thing with their hands.

"Lincoln?" Molly said nervously from beside him.

"I'm thinking," he assured her.

"That's what you said the last time."

"We didn't die, did we?"

She grunted, accepted a brush from Salome who had retaken her seat on the other side of the table, and turned away from him, clearly disturbed that he had not, as yet, lived up to her expectations.

It's a curse, he thought; people these days expect too much of tailors. They see too many movies, read too many books, and then they're crushed when the genuine article can't produce a magical weapon in time to save the day from the hordes of evil overwhelming the land. They even expected him to be tall, dark, and ruggedly handsome, whereas he was actually of medium height, slender, and with undistinguished brown hair that kept falling into his eyes if he didn't use a hair spray.

"Well, you old landlubber," Pigmeo said heartily, "it's about that time!"

He glared, and gripped the armrests more tightly.

"We will, of course, be taxiing to a private section of the airport," the little man informed him gaily. "I think we will have a reception committee."

"Immigration, I hope."

Pigmeo laughed loudly and slapped his thighs, then looked to Salome who managed a tight, mirthless grin. She apparently still hadn't forgiven Lincoln for leaving her in the hotel to be blown to her component parts, and he hadn't been able to convince her that Molly's appearance with the skillet had not been part of his plan.

"What then?" he asked as the plane began to drop.

"Why, then we will seek out Miss Partridge's delightful and clever brother."

"What?" Molly said. "Monty?"

"But of course, my ponytailed one," Pigmeo assured her. "Our instructions are quite clear on that score, isn't that right, my darling?"

Salome shrugged.

"You see?"

"And what about Cull?" Lincoln said, not daring to believe the one-eyed man wouldn't be waiting for them when they landed.

The plane made several adjustments, and he gasped when the pilot—a blond, khaki-uniformed, husky young man—walked around the screen and headed for the cockpit, yawning, stretching, and scratching himself wherever his long fingers could reach in a hurry.

"Oh my god," Molly said when she saw him.

"If he isn't," Lincoln said, "we could be in trouble."

Pigmeo frowned a moment, then burst into a gale of laughter that made Lincoln wince. Even Salome allowed herself a smile, just before she took a stale sandwich from the tray and stuffed it, lovingly, into the little man's mouth. Lincoln appreciated the gesture, but he still scrambled silently for a prayer or two as the water rushed closer, the rolling waves rose higher, and the sun flared through the windows opposite and temporarily blinded him.

When he stopped blinking, the runway was below them, making contact with barely a squeal and almost immediately headed away from the main terminals toward a small hangar shaded by a clutch of palm trees.

Neither Pigmeo nor Testa moved.

Molly leaned across Lincoln to look out the window, and as he pressed away from her to give her room she whispered, "I think we're going to be all right."

"Sure," he said just as quietly.

"No, I mean it."

"Good for you. Stiff upper lip and all that."

She turned awkwardly and glowered at him, pressed back into her own seat, and began humming softly. Salome eyed her suspiciously, but Arturo joined her in expert counterpoint. Lincoln didn't know the tune, and was sure he wouldn't recognize it even if he did; nevertheless, he could not understand why, suddenly, the mood in the cabin had altered so dramatically.

True, they were in Hawaii, the land of beautiful women, beautiful beaches, beautiful foliage, soft nights, and gentle breezes; true, they had landed in one piece, which was a superb testament to those who had created the on-board computers and had let the chips fall where they may; and true, Takana hadn't reached under his seat for the rifle Linc had seen braced there just before the heavy man strapped himself in for the landing.

But Molly was absolutely transfixed.

The plane taxied on, the sun's glare making him squint as he tried to study their surroundings. But except for the palms, the enormous white clouds and stark blue sky, and the short sleeves and pants many of the early morning workers wore, he could have been in almost any tropical airport. So where, he wondered, are all the grass skirts?

Five minutes later they coasted into the relatively cool shadows of the hangar. There was a muffled grinding and a few shudders before the engines wound down with a whine, and the light dimmed as the massive doors slid shut.

Then the cockpit door opened and the pilot returned to the cabin.

Molly stiffened.

Lincoln stiffened in reaction.

Takana unbuckled himself and reached down for the rifle.

That's when the pilot reached into his shirt,

pulled out a gun, and aimed it at the henchman's forehead.

"One move," he said, "and you're sushi."

"I told you he did not look Hawaiian," Salome hissed angrily at Pigmeo, adding a vicious slap to the man's shoulder for emphasis.

Arturo bleated meekly in aggrieved pain and rubbed his wound gingerly with his left hand, while his right reached into his tuxedo jacket.

The pilot pulled another gun from inside his shirt and aimed it at the back of the little man's skull. The sound of the hammer being thumbed back froze Pigmeo and, after a glance for approval, Lincoln reached across the table and took out the gun holstered under the man's arm.

Then he pointed it at the pilot's heart and said, "Who the hell are you?"

"Angel Lymington," Molly told him cheerfully, unfastening her seat belt and springing to her feet. She stretched, grinned, and blew a kiss at their rescuer.

The pilot saluted her, British-fashion.

"And who the hell is Angel Lymington?" Lincoln asked, lowering his arm but still not rising.

"RAF, retired," the pilot said stiffly. "And I'll thank you, sir, to please prepare yourself for departure before the others get here."

"Others?"

Molly grabbed his arm and yanked him to his feet, then rushed into the galley and returned with a length of twine she used to tie Testa and Pigmeo in their seats. Meanwhile, Lymington fetched the rifle from under Takana's seat, cradled it under his arm, and walked behind the screen.

"What the hell's going on?" Lincoln demanded.

"Beats me," Takana told him, eyeing the gun in Linc's hand and deciding it still wasn't a good time to practice the lethal movements his hands had been trained for over the past twenty years. "That guy was hiding down below when I went there, after you were supposed to be dead. I thought he worked for Mr. Cull."

"I thought he worked for you."

"I work for no one, sir," Lymington announced as he returned with several sheets torn into strips. As he bound Takana into his seat, he explained tersely that he had been hired by Mr. Partridge to keep an eye out for potential interference, for he feared he would find himself in serious trouble as he continued with his current research. To do this, it was necessary to incapacitate the plane's original pilot and take his place without notice. That bit of sleight of hand had taken place after the prisoners had been brought aboard.

As for Miss Partridge, he had known her since she was a child, though he hadn't seen her in many years.

There was a muffled thump outside. Lincoln guessed it was a portable staircase being positioned against the plane.

Once Takana was securely in place, grumbling and eyeing them all with simmering fury, Lymington sighed and dropped his weapons into the nearest seat. Then he took a massive yellowed and torn handkerchief from his hip pocket, shook it out and began to rub at his face vigorously. Though it was increasingly warm in the cabin, Lincoln didn't see the need for such a thorough going-over until, when the handkerchief lowered, he saw the man's face.

"Well, damn and double-damn. I thought you were a bit young to be retired."

Lymington, once his expertly applied makeup was removed and the handkerchief replaced, bowed and smiled. "I'll be sixty-one come December, sir. Keep myself in shape."

Someone pounded on the exit door.

Molly tied towel-gags around the mouths of their prisoners, then gathered up the weapons and distributed them with appropriate comments on their efficacy. She then gestured Lincoln into the seat nearest the door, took the one behind him, and nodded to the pilot, who took a deep breath, smoothed down his uniform, cranked open the door, and stepped back deferentially, with his gun hidden by his right side.

The air that rushed in was hot, extremely humid, and Salome whimpered in dismay as her hair began to curl visibly.

Loop Molahu strode in, nodded curtly to Lymington, and glared at Molly and Lincoln. Then his eyes widened when he saw his partner trussed and gagged, widened farther when he saw Pigmeo and Testa across the cabin.

He whirled. "What the hell?"

Lymington pointed the gun at Molahu's nose. "Good morning," he said.

Molahu slapped the gun away and landed a massive and well-practiced fist against the pilot's chin. Lymington spun back through the door, grabbing wildly for the handrail as he slid and stumbled down the metal steps. Before Molahu could turn back, Linc was on his feet and had his arms around the man's chest, wrestling with him, dodging well-aimed heels, and looking to Molly for assistance.

Molly, however, was busy staring at the window.

Well, hell, he thought, and maneuvered Molahu to the open door, positioned a knee into his rump, and shoved. Molahu reached desperately for the frame; Lincoln brought the side of his hand sharply onto his elbow; Molahu pitched forward, and fell. One step at a time. Landing across an unconscious Lymington's legs.

"Out," he ordered.

Molly obeyed without further prompting, and they rushed down the steps, dumped Molahu onto his side and between them managed to carry Lymington to a small door in the building's rear. A quick glance back to be sure they weren't being followed, and they plunged through, into the already stifling island morning.

FIFTEEN

THE SEVENTH INN OF THE ANCIENT PALMS, FAR OFF
the beaten track and definitely not in downtown
Honolulu, was losing its inferior pastel paint in
great swatches from its leaning stuccoed walls. Its
pink facade faced a narrow, cluttered street lined
with tiny shops, unsavory bars, and doorways
where men lounged in tight pants and young
women in tighter sarongs with zippers down the
front were already poised for swift execution.

Once through the high wooden door in the Inn's
not very imposing center wall, however, one discovered a small courtyard dominated by grass that
badly needed cutting, a massive mango tree growing out of a chipped fountain with a green stone
dolphin in its bowl, and a dozen doors facing a dark
red slate walk that served as the courtyard's bound-
ary. The office was in back, its sorry condition in-
dicative of its usual clientele.

Lincoln had booked Cabin Ten, in the left rear
corner, with a clear view of the entrance through
the mango and the high grass. Inside were two
double beds whose linen was almost as thin as the
mattresses, one dresser, one unprejudiced televi-

sion that knew no color, an air-conditioning unit that worked in spite of the constant dripping, and a bathroom whose tiled walls and floor were entirely pink.

Lymington lay on the bed farther from the door, still unconscious. His khaki shirt had been opened to the waist, there was a damp washcloth over his forehead, and he was snoring.

Molly sat on the other bed resetting her ponytail while Lincoln stood at the venetian blinds and peered out from behind a pair of oversized sunglasses.

"This is not what I expected Honolulu to be like," she said glumly. "You must have different brochures or something."

"Honolulu is not for tourists," he told her without turning around. "Tourist money never filters down this far. Most of that stays in the big hotels over at Waikiki."

"It's dirty!"

"It's unpleasant," he said, making a fine distinction he didn't think she'd understand.

"There's a small army of prostitutes outside, and pimps, and illegal gambling operations that take cruel advantage of the poor and unread."

"Blame it on the missionaries," he said. "They made the women wear bras. And I still haven't seen a grass skirt."

"Plastic."

"I don't care, as long as one of them moves in the right direction."

She closed one eye and glared at him. "You are disgusting."

"I didn't get a moose, why can't I have one simple grass skirt?"

She slumped against the headboard and crossed her legs Indian fashion. "And you haven't even made a pass at me."

"I—" He stopped, took off the sunglasses, and gave his forehead a three-finger massage.

"You probably like that Testa woman," she said, pouting. "In her tight green dress and all that hair and all that . . ." She fluttered a hand over her own chest.

"She's not unattractive," he admitted ruefully.

She made a gesture that indicated he should reexamine his parentage, make allowances for his unnatural state of grace, and generally bugger off.

Lincoln thought to seek a way to make amends, decided that she would break his jaw if he tried, and looked back to the outside when the outer door opened and a young woman with long black hair hurried in with a corpulent, sweating, red-faced, supremely embarrassed man in tow. They disappeared into the first cabin. They came out ten minutes later. The man's face was redder, he was sweating more, and he kept one hand shading his eyes while the woman kissed his cheek, pulled up her sarong zipper and put on her spiked red shoes.

She'd do better with a grass skirt, he thought.

He said, "We can't stay here long. Those gentlemen at the airport won't waste much time getting loose and coming after us."

"How are they going to find us in this place?"

"Hard work and determination."

She harrumphed.

"What we have to do is find your brother before they do."

"Then let's go! If we can find him first, we can keep them from finding him and stop them from finding out what he's really up to, which we'll know because we'll have found him already and can find a place to hide him."

But neither of them moved.

Molly wasn't going to leave her old family friend alone in this place, unconscious though in fine shape, and Lincoln knew that if he himself didn't get some sleep and soon, he'd start seeing double.

On the other hand, delaying until they were rested would mean that many hours Cull's men were ahead of him.

Still, if they knew where Montague was, they wouldn't have bothered with him and Molly in the first place; therefore, they had to find him and Molly in order to make him tell them where Monty was, even though he didn't know, and Jesus, now he was even thinking the way she talked.

All in all, however, and for the sake of his deteriorating mental alertness, he decided it was a safe bet they could take three or four hours off, sleep and get something decent to eat, and move out.

"Where," he said, "is your brother?"

"I don't know."

He watched the deserted courtyard for several seconds more before taking a seat at the foot of the bed. "What do you mean, you don't know?"

She looked down into her lap and watched her hands. "Well, not exactly."

"Okay."

"I mean, I know he's in this state someplace."

"That narrows it down to about eight major islands and a bunch of rocks in the water."

"And I guess he'll be where the volcanos are."

"Hawaii."

"That's where we are."

"I mean, the island of Hawaii."

"Aren't we there?"

"We're on Oahu."

"In Hawaii."

"Right," he said.

"Oh. I get it."

"Good. Now, where on Hawaii do you think he is?"

"I don't know. I've never been here before." Then she brightened. "But Angel will know! He works for Monty."

Relieved, he nodded without saying another word and toed off his boots, unbuttoned his shirt and lay down, pushing Molly over with a wave of his hand. She looked perplexedly at him for a long time until he explained that rushing off at the height of weariness was not the best way to save her brother from Cull. And as long as Cull was as much in the dark as they were, they could afford to get some rest.

"But Cull will know about the volcanos."

"But Hawaii, my dear, is a very large island, with more forest than you can shake a stick at. Unless he knows precisely where Monty is, which he does not, he won't find him before we do."

"What if he gets lucky?"

He rolled his head over on the thin pillow and

looked up at her, considered keeping silent, and decided it would do no good.

"If he does find him, Molly, I know where to go next."

"Where's that?"

His hesitation made her ask the question again, this time a bit more apprehensively.

"Kampollea."

"Where's that?"

"It's not a where, it's a what."

"What is it, then?"

"An island."

"Where's that?"

"West of here. It's not," he said quickly, "on most maps. It's what you might call a perfect example of private enterprise at work."

"What? Lincoln, what are you talking about?"

"Kampollea," he said, "is what you might call Florenz Cull's private torture chamber."

The island is slightly less than four miles across and almost completely circular. From passing ships it is a forbidding jumble of dark rocks rising almost a thousand feet above the surface, its sides disturbed only by noisy colonies of seabirds, and by a few areas of tenacious plant life that add the only green; three shallow depressions are used for beaching purposes, though there is no sand and the water is instantly too deep and treacherous for swimming. From above, one can see the gentle inland slopes covered with tropical jungle-like growth, and in the center a small lake that reflects the mood of the sky. There is no sign of habitation, no airstrips, no visible roads—the forest canopy covers everything but the water.

At night there are no lights, and the lake is black.

At night the sound of the ocean battering the cliffs is a distant thunderstorm that never arrives.

And at night there is a fog that lifts from the cool water to sift into the trees, to curl around the legs of strollers on paths that stretch from the slopes to the series of palm-thatched buildings on the lake's northern shore. Oddly, the fog is warm; not so oddly, it carries a faint odor of sulphur, brought with it from the water where no living creature exists, not even the hardiest of shellfish which may find their way there through the underground, undersea passages that keep the lake filled.

Once or twice a year, the lake writhes like a cauldron.

Polynesian explorers, having landed there once, called it Kampollea, the Heart of the Beast, and never returned.

Lincoln slept for eight hours without moving, dozed for one more, and finally opened his eyes. The sun was low in the western sky, the shadows filling the courtyard and giving it a tropical elegance it would never have in full daylight. He yawned, stretched his arms over his head, and looked to his right. Molly was there, still sleeping, as was Lymington in the other bed.

Carefully, he eased off the mattress and went into the bathroom, took a look at himself in the mirror, and decided he did not look good in a beard. In fact, he looked like a man who hadn't shaved in several days, hadn't slept in a week, and hadn't been culturally attuned to the civilized world for most of his natural, adult life.

"You look like hell, Blackthorne," he said as he located the soap, turned on the water, and proceeded to give himself as good a wash as he could. He had already checked out the shower stall and decided that whatever was flourishing in the corners must be first cousin to whatever had been growing in the hotel in Maine; and since he wasn't a biologist, or an aficionado of fungus, he settled for the sink.

Fifteen minutes later he thought he might pass for a spruced-up Robinson Crusoe and went into the other room. Molly was awake and sitting beside Lymington, whose eyelids were fluttering their way back into the world.

Lincoln checked the courtyard again, closed the blinds, and said, "How is he?"

"Better."

"Good. We have to move as soon as he can get up."

Molly nodded, and lightly patted the old man's cheek. When he didn't respond, she slapped him. "I don't believe in coddling the elderly," she explained after the retired RAF pilot had leapt to his feet, shadowboxed the headboard, and disappeared into the bathroom. "It only lulls them into a false sense of security which, at their age, can be extremely dangerous. They have to learn to live on their own, be self-sufficient, and be productive members of society as best they can, being a downtrodden minority without much political savvy or power."

153

"I see. So you slapped him."

"Oh that. No, that was because he pinched my chest."

An eyebrow lifted, but he said nothing.

"Anyway, I'm ready when you are."

Water ran in the shower stall, and he thought the man a braver soul than he.

"Why is he called Angel?"

"Because he flies."

"A lot of pilots do, but I never heard any of them with a name like that."

"Well, actually, he wasn't very good."

Lincoln sniffed.

"I guess you could say he was awfully unlucky."

He cleared his throat.

"He's probably very lucky to be alive."

He sighed.

"And he's not actually retired. They sort of asked him to leave before the Germans found out he was on our side." She smiled quickly then. "But don't say anything, all right? It would hurt his feelings."

And that, he thought, took care of his plan to find a private plane and have Lymington fly them to Hawaii.

The water ran on in the shower.

Molly rose and knocked politely on the door. "Angel?"

Lincoln walked over and knocked as well. "Hey, Angel!"

Molly said, "He's gonna be a prune."

Lincoln opened the door, batted away the steam that flowed out of the room, and yanked aside the plastic shower curtain. The stall was empty. He wasn't surprised. Nor was he surprised when he found the pebble-glass window opened onto a dirt alley in back.

Molly called him.

You old fart, he thought, and strode into the front room where Molly was kneeling in front of the television.

"We haven't time," he said, heading for the door. "We've got to get him before he leaves the island on his own."

"Lincoln."

"Molly, for heaven's sake!"

"Lincoln, look."

He looked.

He saw an early evening news show.

He saw a film clip, no doubt very colorful. Fire. Sparks. A man in a park ranger's uniform talking to a reporter.

"Hell," he said.

"It's Mauna Loa," she said quietly. "The third worst eruption of the century, and the lava flow's heading straight for Hilo."

SIXTEEN

DUE TO THE UNWIELDY AND SOMEWHAT SCATTERED nature of the state's geographical structure—parts of it being, as they were, separated from other parts by the Pacific Ocean—there are perforce a number of flourishing and accommodating private airlines which delight in island-hopping for a suitable fee, a fair amount of private charter concerns which disdain the air for the sea itself for a suitable fee, and a few very private companies whose business is known only to a limited number of people, none of whom work for the federal government. The fee may not be democratically suitable, but one pays for what one asks for.

Lincoln held Molly's hand, then, as they walked through a winding series of back streets, eventually finding themselves in a milieu neither seen by nor explained to the island's visitors, such an explanation being generally considered to be bad for business and the state's innocent yet exotic image. She complained the entire way about her feet, the enervating press of tropical heat, and the way some rather good-looking young men kept staring at her as if she were a slab of tourist steak about to be well-done; she also wondered why they weren't combing the streets for Lymington since he was, when all was said and done, in just as much danger as they were.

Lincoln, on the other hand, by his determined stride and the angle of his head, prevented anyone from approaching them. He wasn't worried about the retired pilot; the old man was probably already on Hawaii, and probably already with Montague. He was primarily concerned with not being side-tracked again by Molahu or Takana, though he suspected that Cull had them, too, on Hawaii for the search.

He wasn't worried.

Unless Cull managed to do something remarkably stupid, Hawaii was not going to be the last stop on this trip.

By eight o'clock they finally reached a string of small, seedy stores set in a cluttered street not much wider than a healthy alley. Molly pressed closer, noting that they were the only Caucasians within ear- and scream-shot, noting too that the area's dim light was not relieved at all by the proliferation of small neon signs which hung over display windows curiously bereft of wares anyone in his right mind would wish to purchase.

They stopped midway to the next block.

Molly looked at the faded gold lettering on the window she faced. "It figures," she said.

Lincoln shrugged.

"I mean, you guys must have a network or something, right? You've banded together into a world-wide conspiracy that fights for the rights of the common man, and woman, to survive in an environment hostile to one's continuing on a normal plane of existence."

"Molly," he said, "the day I understand one word of what you say is the day I turn in my chalk and ruler."

She pointed at the window, in which were two mannequins, one wearing a frilly white dress and carrying a parasol, the other in a sleek white suit and wearing a straw boater.

"That," she announced, "is a tailor shop."

He knocked on the door. "Right."

"You are a tailor."

He knocked again. "Right."

She spread her arms as if her point were proven, then grabbed his hand tightly when the door opened and a small, deep voice invited them in.

There was a spacious room in back of the store decorated in fond memory of Sidney Greenstreet, and with a touch of Peter Lorre, complete with throne-backed wicker chairs, slow-spinning ceiling fans, palm fronds in the corners, and a massive teak desk in front of a high shuttered window. Behind the desk was a man, evidently Japanese in heritage and with a taste for the richer foods the Occidentals have to offer. He wore a rumpled white suit, no tie, and in his gnarled right hand he held an empty ivory cigarette holder. He nodded politely when Lincoln entered the room, rose gracefully when Molly followed close behind, and gestured them both to seats facing him.

When Molly was introduced he said nothing beyond a grunt that may or may not have been an appreciation of her appearance. Then he sat again, examined the tip of his holder, and flicked a lazy hand at the air, in the general direction of a standing gold bird cage in which a brilliantly colored parrot sat on its perch and contemplated the fans.

"Lincoln Blackthorne, a pleasure," the heavy man said.

"It's been a while, Sol Norkuro."

"Too long."

"Funny. I was going to say not long enough."

The man laughed silently, exposing an upper plate in dire need of massive repair. "Do you wish refreshment?"

"Thank you, Sol, but I'd prefer transportation."

"Ah. And where do you wish to go?"

"Hawaii."

"You're already here."

"The island," Linc said, looking hard at Molly to see if there was any family resemblance.

Molly ignored him; she was too busy examining the parrot, trying to figure out what it was staring at.

"Air?" Norkuro lifted the empty holder then, and shook his head with a regretful smile. "Never mind. My memory failed me for the moment. A boat."

"Please."

Norkuro closed his eyes, tented his fingers beneath his chin, and hummed monotonically. A few seconds later he nodded, and struck a small gong beside his desk. It was out of tune. Linc winced as a door opened in the righthand wall and a young Hawaiian stepped through. He was husky, clean-shaven, and wore a blinding white shirt that hung outside a pair of equally blinding white trousers.

"Mr. Blackthorne!" he exclaimed with pleasure when he recognized the visitor. "Wow!"

"Thomas Olakani," Linc said to Molly, "knows me. I'm a good tipper."

"Thomas," Norkuro said stiffly, "you will refrain from such exhibitions and prepare a launch for our friend."

"Wow!"

"He wants to go to the big island."

"Oh . . . wow."

Norkuro sighed. "Thomas has heard of the eruption, I think. And I wonder if you have too, Mr. Blackthorne."

"I won't be going to Hilo, Sol."

Norkuro held up the holder again—he did not want an itinerary, not even a negative one. Then he held out his free hand, palm up, and Lincoln pulled from his shirt the packet of Salome's money he'd been protecting since he'd left Maine. A few bills were counted out, a few more when the Japanese frowned, and one more when Norkuro cleared his throat.

"Inflation," the man explained as the money was deftly folded and placed into his jacket pocket.

"If you say so."

"Lincoln," Molly said in a loud whisper.

"Thomas will now take you to the boat."

"Yessir, right away," Thomas said, hustling over to stand beside the old man and listen to a series of soft, guttural instructions. He nodded once, blanched twice, and three times made to shake his head. Norkuro hissed at him. Thomas shrugged, resigned to the recognition of his own mortality.

Molly leaned around the wrap of her wicker chair and tapped Lincoln's arm. "Lincoln, that parrot over there."

He looked. "Yep, that's a parrot."

"It's dead."

He looked harder. "Yep, I guess it is."

She glanced at the Japanese and the Hawaiian still in earnest conversation. "But who keeps a dead parrot in a cage?"

"A man who values beauty and silence."

Norkuro dismissed Thomas with a curt wave, and rose.

Lincoln stood. Norkuro held out his hand, took Molly's, and bowed over it. He murmured something in Japanese and Molly smiled. Thomas tapped his foot impatiently at the door, and Lincoln, who didn't know that Molly understood the language, took her arm and led her from the room. Thomas immediately hurried in front and led them out of the shop through a back entrance, down an alley strewn with garbage and parked Mercedes, around a corner into another alley, and down a long street packed with pedestrians out for a cool night's stroll.

The noise level was high, and Linc made no effort to talk, since it would have involved a certain amount of shouting; he did, however, keep an eye on the rooftops, the faces of the pedestrians, and his back. He was beginning to think that perhaps he had made a mistake in waiting so long to find Montague; on the other hand, he did feel better for the sleep, and smiled at wishes transformed to deeds when Thomas ducked into a shop and returned with a bag filled with groceries.

The streets began to empty.

As the sun dropped below the roofline, shadows replaced the population, and though Honolulu glowed brightly behind them, wiping out most of the stars and the romance, it was dark enough at street level for Lincoln to grow increasingly nervous.

Molly, who had been chatting with Thomas, dropped back and hugged his arm. "He's very interesting," she whispered with a nod toward the young man's back.

"He is that."

"He says he knows you from a long time ago."

"True."

"He wouldn't tell me how, though. I think, if you want to know the truth, he's hiding something."

"It must be the boat," Lincoln said with a scowl, "because I'll be damned if I know what the hell he's up to. We should have been there by now." Then he grinned. "From my lips to Norkuro's ears."

They stepped around a low white building and found themselves facing a spawling marina. Thomas took them to the left, onto a long wharf lined with expensive, gleaming craft larger than most hotel rooms Lincoln had seen. The water was calm, the salt sharp in the air, and a few late-flying gulls wheeled raucously overhead. Radios from some of the docked sloops and cabin cruisers filled the air with rock music, Hawaiian music, Oriental music, and a furtive bit of Mozart.

Molly seemed subdued by the ostentatious opulence that surrounded her as she gawked at the varied boats in unabashed wonder. Several times she moved to the end of a walkway to peer into a convenient porthole, or at a riotous party being thrown beneath strings of Chinese lanterns on someone's deck. And each time she did she shook her head slowly.

Lincoln did not share her amazement for the pursuits of the wealthy and the pretenders; he was too busy paying attention to those boats which were dark, and to those passengers he thought eyed them too closely for simple idle curiosity. Suspicion, he knew, was the bane of his existence, yet he was unable to shake the feeling that he had gotten off much too lightly since their flight from the airport.

Much too lightly indeed.

Were he not an already suspicious man, he would have been converted hours ago.

As they reached the end of the wharf, he glanced behind him and saw a shadowed man standing at the far end with his hands in his pockets. He had no idea who the watcher was, but he didn't like the cold that pricked the back of his neck.

He stopped, and soon Thomas and Molly were at his side.

"Golly," Thomas muttered.

"Who is he?" Molly asked, following Lincoln's gaze.

The shadowed man began to walk toward them.

"I haven't the slightest idea."

"What'll we do?"

"Find out what he's selling, and not buy anything."

"Wow," Thomas whispered, and hitched up his white trousers, smoothed down his white shirt, and started walking himself.

Lincoln, with a touch of his hand, ordered Molly to stay where she was, then shifted to the right side of the pier and kept pace with Thomas ten feet behind. He rolled his shoulders to ease the tension, felt for the knife at his wrist to be sure it was still there, and did his best not to trip over the lines curled on the boarding.

The parties continued.

No one paid them any mind.

The shadowed man stepped through a patch of flickering light, and Lincoln saw that he was dressed entirely in black, from the seaman's cap on his head to the sneakers on his feet. His right hand swung easily at his side, his left was in his hip pocket.

Thomas walked as if he were out for a stroll.

This isn't right, Lincoln thought; if I'm wrong, we're going to look like idiots, and if I'm not, that guy is an idiot for coming alone.

Then he heard a faint splash to his left, between the stern of a deserted yacht and the prow of its double. He froze, listened, and dropped slowly into a crouch. Thomas, if he'd heard, did not react but continued on his way, and Lincoln scuttled across the boards to grab onto the top of a piling around which a mooring rope had been wound. He leaned over the side, and snapped back before a similarly dark-attired man climbing out of a rubber raft could see him.

Thomas stopped.

The shadowed man stopped.

Thomas nodded casually.

The shadowed man cocked his head and stared.

A woman in a rather casual state of undress ran squealing from a boat to the wharf, followed by a man waving a shirt in one hand and a halter top in another. They wound drunkenly around the two men, laughing, nearly tripping, finally streaking back to their home base with great whoops of delight.

Marvelous what the night air will do, Lincoln thought, and blinked when he realized he was staring at the coarse, tanned fingers of someone's brazen hand gripping the edge of the dock at his feet. Sneering at his shadow for allowing himself to be distracted by cheap thrills, he considered a moment before standing suddenly, lifting his heel and bringing it down hard across the first row of knuckles.

The man below howled.

The shadowed man whipped his left hand around.

Thomas spun, kicked, and caught the left wrist before it was able to release a long-bladed knife.

Lincoln looked over the edge to see the shadowed man's companion paddling frantically away in the rubber boat; when he looked to Thomas, the shadowed man was racing toward shore, his left arm cradled against his chest.

The half-naked woman came to the railing of her sloop and demanded they either pipe down or join the party but stop ruining other people's birthdays.

Thomas and Molly reached Lincoln at the same time and followed his pointing finger.

"Golly," Thomas said.

"You did pretty well yourself," Linc told him.

"Who were they?" Molly asked.

Lincoln gave her a *don't ask stupid questions* look, and suggested they move on before someone else came along to interrupt their trip. Thomas agreed, but hesitated just long enough for Linc to give him a look.

"Are . . ." The young man looked to Molly apologetically. "Are we in for another one of those things, Mr. Blackthorne?"

"Could be."

He shook his head sadly. "Wow."

"What things?" Molly asked fearfully, then held up her hands; she didn't want to know.

Good, Lincoln thought, because then I'd have to tell her about the man with the rifle standing behind her.

SEVENTEEN

A SINGLE HARD LOOK TO THOMAS, AND THE HAWAI-
ian immediately put himself between the rifleman
and Molly, at the same time taking her arm and
ushering her gently away. Meanwhile, Lincoln
raised his left hand as if to scratch his cheek, flexed
the proper muscles and felt the abrupt release of a
well-coiled spring.

The knife leapt from its sheath with only a minor
tearing of the sleeve's cuff.

There was a grunt from the shadows on the deck
across the way.

Molly wondered aloud what in god's name was
going on, but Thomas didn't give her a chance to
follow when Lincoln hurried across the dock,
vaulted onto the boat and retrieved his knife from
the man's chest. He peered closely at the body, did
not recognize the man, and wiped the blade
thoughtfully on the corpse's black shirt.

This game, he thought, is getting too damned
crowded.

After reinserting the weapon into its hidden
sheath, he rolled the body to the deck's far side,
checked up and down the length of the wharf to be

sure he wasn't being watched, then toed the man's waist distastefully until he slipped over the side and into the bay. Then he turned and hurriedly followed the others to the end of the wharf. There, taking up a berth more suited to a destroyer, was a motor yacht named the *Hari Kiri XIII* which, he estimated, could easily have slept thirty in a pinch. With a silent and appreciative nod to Norkuro and his accommodations, and a definite reservation about the name, he clambered aboard just as Thomas climbed to the bridge and entered the wheelhouse where Linc saw another man turn, smile a greeting, tilt his head to listen to instructions, and nod once.

It was obvious the seaman had only one arm; it was just as obvious that he didn't require two.

"Our captain," he said to Molly, who appeared at his side.

"If he has one leg I'm going to scream."

"Relax. There isn't anything we can do now until we reach the island."

She looked doubtfully at him, but wandered around the spacious deck until she located a trio of canvas-backed chairs facing the squared stern across a low table bolted to the flooring. She sat heavily, and he took a seat beside her. Behind them, in almost total silence, they could hear footsteps running here and there as the crew prepared for castoff.

A faint breeze blew in off the bay.

A bell sounded three times, and ropes splashed into the water.

"Lincoln," she said, "I don't mind telling you I'm a little nervous about this."

"So am I."

"What I mean to say is, I don't know if I'm up to killing Cull when I see him."

He nodded without looking at her. "You never did tell me why he murdered your father."

"No, I didn't."

"Are you?" he asked after a suitable interval.

She swallowed hard, and pushed at the hair the breeze kept fanning across her eyes. "Do you know the story?"

"Yes, part of it," and he told her what Salome had told him in the hotel room by the river. By the time he had finished, the cruiser had already moved away from its berth, and they were heading out to sea.

"I see," Molly said. "Well, after the war, my father, still a very young man but very brilliant, was put in charge of unscrambling the government archeologists' notes. He was the one who had discovered the so-called powers the Soldier had. And he was the one Cull came after."

"Why?"

"My father told him," she answered bitterly. "He didn't know Cull then—they were both young men, but my father younger than most. He trusted too much."

"So Cull killed him."

"No. Cull stole the notes and ran off. My father chased him for many months, finally catching him somewhere in central Europe."

He nodded his understanding.

"No," she said. "Not then. They decided to become partners, to each use their unique talents to search out this statuette and test it."

Oh dear, Lincoln thought.

"That in itself took many years more."

He looked at Molly, at the beautiful hair and soft, undemanding profile, and wondered if perhaps he'd gotten into the game on the wrong side.

"But they found it, although apparently, before they had a chance to test it, my father took it and ran off. I think he knew, at last, what the limitations of the Soldier's power were, and he didn't like them. He changed his identity, had plastic surgery, and met and married my mother. He settled down in Wisconsin, which is where . . . which is where Cull found him, and killed him."

"But Cull doesn't have the Soldier."

"No, Monty does." She frowned. "I thought you knew that."

"I do, but how did Monty get it?"

"He stole it from my father."

"Oh. All right." He sat back and watched the wake trail whitely behind them. "I hate to ask this, but do you have any idea who killed the men who found the statuette in the first place?"

"Sure."

"I was afraid of that. Your father, right?"

"For heaven's sake, Lincoln, no. He was much too young then. It was my uncle. His older brother."

"I think," he said, "I'm going to have the captain turn this boat around."

There was no time for Molly to learn if he were kidding or not. Thomas climbed out of the companionway with a small silver tray in hand. He offered them each a drink of his own special blends of rum, orange juice, and secret ingredients and suggested a light meal which Lincoln approved, and disappeared again.

Molly looked after him. "Is he a servant or what?"

"He's an 'or what.' "

Her eyes were narrow over the rim of her glass.

"He does what he's told."

The eyes widened.

"Right," he said. "Beneath that youthful, handsome face and scintillating conversational technique, he's a wonderfully skilled technician."

"Of what?" she said, her mouth plugged with an ice cube.

"Don't ask."

"Wow," she said softly, and turned her attention back to the wake that foamed and fanned a startling white in the dark water. The engines were barely audible, the increasing size of the waves barely felt as they breached the harbor's mouth and swung slowly north, toward the big island. The engines raised their workload, and the stern settled a bit deeper in the water, the wind grew a bit stronger, and it wasn't long before the glittering lights of Honolulu, Pearl Harbor, and Oahu were drifting lazily toward the horizon.

They had a journey of over two hundred and fifty miles—taking into consideration the certain time-tested avoidance techniques the captain would be taking to prevent their untimely disclosure. Despite the fact that he had already slept most of the day away, Lincoln soon felt a pleasant weariness slip over him. He yawned. Molly yawned. They took their drinks below and sat in an expansive, just shy of palatial cabin, now handsomely laid out for dinner for two.

It may well have been the most delicious meal he had ever eaten, but the gentle roll of the cruiser, and the wine, and the sparkling soft lights glinting off the brass, the polished wood, and Molly's eyes, lulled him further until, at last, he suggested they get some rest.

She declared she was wide-awake and intended to do some stargazing.

He declared that he was not wide-awake, didn't much care to look at stars, and certainly didn't care to look at stars reflected in water that was a good deal deeper than the top of his head.

She pouted.

He shrugged, and found his stateroom, found his bunk already turned down, and found the light switch.

When a distant scolding erupted somewhere in a foggy part of his brain, he told himself that he was not, no matter how it looked, lying down on the job.

The last thing he heard before falling asleep was Molly on the deck outside his porthole, giggling, while Thomas said, "Wow."

The yacht anchored in a remote cove off the southwest coast of Maui for several hours in order to give the skeleton crew a rest. They moved on shortly after dawn, at a much slower pace now which, Thomas explained, would not bring them any unwanted attention from the government boats which had begun patrolling the coastal waters since Mauna Loa first erupted. Too many tourists and locals, he explained, wanted to see the excitement from the sea, and the danger wasn't from the eruptions as much as it was from careless drivers.

Lincoln, though anxious to get on with it, approved.

"Lincoln?" Molly asked some time later.

"What?"

"You're getting a sunburn. I think you ought to get a shirt on or get under an umbrella or something."

"I know. I never tan, you know. I get burned, I peel, and then I get burned again. I hate people who tan without agony. It's unnatural."

"I tan easily. If I stay out here long enough, I'll start to look like a native."

"I'm going below before I get into a shotgun wedding with a lobster."

He rose from the chair, caped his shirt around his shoulders, and hissed when the soft cloth touched what felt like a griddle attached to his bones.

Molly grinned and turned her head, pointing to the deck. "It looks broken."

"You mean all those lines?"

"Yes. Almost like a jigsaw puzzle. I've been making pictures out of them, like you do when you look at clouds. Is it a special kind of wood?"

"Not really. It's a special kind of deck."

"What kind is that?"

"I don't know. Ask Thomas."

"I did. He told me not to ask."

"Then don't."

She threw an ice cube at him and stared glumly at the sea, which was almost too bright to look at even with the sunglasses Thomas had provided for them.

"Did you hear the radio this morning?" she said as he turned to go below.

"I was sleeping this morning."

"You were sleeping this noon, too."

"I need my rest."

"You look—"

"What about the radio?"

"Mauna Loa has stopped erupting."

"Good news!"

"The lava flow will probably stop before it reaches the outskirts of the city."

"Better news!"

"Boy, you're in a good mood all of a sudden."

"Good news always puts me in a good mood. It tells me not to despair, that life is worth living after all."

"What if I told you that Kilauea erupted just after ten?"

"Damn!"

"That's what I thought you'd say."

He stood on the foredeck, Thomas stolid beside him, Hawaii ahead—rising green and massive out of the swells, a shifting dark cloud hovering over it as though half of the unseen slopes were burning to the ground. They had swung considerably north in the past hour, well clear of the channel that separated the big island from Maui, heading for another remote cove in the least patrolled and inhabited section of the national park. A few small aircraft circled the island; a number of large and small boats were hugging the shoreline.

"Two hours," Thomas informed him.

"Fine," Lincoln said.

Thomas snapped his fingers.

Lincoln waited for the question.

"Am I to go ashore with you?"

"Do you want to?"

"No," the young man said quickly, then ducked his head in shame.

"Thomas," he chided, "don't tell me you don't trust me."

"I have been with you once, remember?"

He did, and he couldn't help a laugh which he kept up even though Molly came scampering around to join them, one arm cautioning them to silence, the other trying to keep herself from pitching overboard.

"Lincoln," she said breathlessly, "I think there's someone following us."

"Are you sure?"

"As sure as I'm standing here, waiting for you to stop standing there and get moving."

Thomas immediately ran aft without further prodding, while Lincoln swore mildly and took Molly below. In the main cabin he found an ornate chest which contained a number of well-kept weapons wrapped in oiled cloth. He handed her a beautifully balanced revolver which she instantly opened in order to inspect the chamber, then snapped shut with a deft flick of her wrist and tucked into her waistband.

He stared.

"A girl has to learn to protect herself when she's on her own in the world," she explained. Then she stared at the gun. "Do you think there's going to be trouble?"

"Precautions."

"Suppose they're only fishermen?"

"Then we don't have trouble."

She walked past him to the stairwell, climbed, and poked her head out. "Lincoln?"

I am getting to hate the way she says that, he thought.

"What?"

"How much trouble are we in if there's a little man on the deck of that boat back there, wearing a tuxedo and singing?"

EIGHTEEN

THE BOAT WAS NEARLY THE SAME SIZE AS NORKURO'S, and hung off to starboard a hundred yards behind, making no attempt to disguise its purpose. Arturo Pigmeo stood tuxedoed at the prow, his arms akimbo, his voice, bellowing Arthur Godfrey through a megaphone, faint over the roar of the engines. Salome was nowhere in sight, but Lincoln didn't think she would have remained ashore, nor did he think they were in any immediate danger, despite the cannon bolted to the foredeck.

"That thing looks like a howitzer," Molly said, blinking her disbelief.

"Close enough."

"Then you don't think he's going to shoot us?"

"Art? No. He just wants to look impressive."

"What is he going to do then?"

"Find out where we're landing."

"Can't he be more subtle?"

Lincoln had no chance to answer. The cruiser's engines revved suddenly to full ahead, and they plowed through the low swells toward the island. Pigmeo dropped behind. Lincoln returned to the cabin and sat at a narrow mahogany table, looking out a porthole at Hawaii and wondering about all the other craft he saw littering the water. It was possible the captain was doing exactly as he was supposed to, and it was also possible that among those scores of inquisitive tourists and natives was someone with a high-powered rifle and an unfortunately expert aim.

The thought made him slump a little lower in his seat.

"He's getting closer," Molly called.

The cruiser slowed as it neared the first boat, a forty-foot sloop on whose decks a sedate party was in progress. Slower, and the people waved their glasses, their leis, and a few acres of tanning, oil-slick flesh. He appreciated the display, but was more pleased when the number of boats increased. Though it forced the *Hari Kiri XIII* to slow down even more, it also prevented Pigmeo from getting any nearer.

Now all he had to worry about was the potential rifleman.

"He's stopped singing," Molly told him cheerfully. "And they've draped something over that cannon or whatever it is."

The cruiser cut speed yet again to avoid swamping some of the smaller boats in its wake, and they were soon passing in front of the mouth of Hilo's harbor. Here it looked as if a boat convention was in progress, and he wasn't surprised.

There, rising over the small city, was the bulk of Mauna Loa, and on its far slope a billowing of smoke from the Kilauea crater. If it were night, he knew he'd be able to see threads of lethal red worming their way down the slopes.

Molly had joined Thomas and the captain in the wheelhouse, and he considered going too. That notion, however, he discarded as soon as he saw Pigmeo's boat some fifty yards away, passing between a pair of catamarans. He saw no evidence of exposed weaponry, but he didn't want to risk it. Instead, he watched carefully, and in fifteen minutes realized that the captain's erratic course around the harbor was positioning the little man's craft for the worst possible pursuit.

The engines surged once, and faded.

He rose and went on deck, leaning against the cabin wall and glancing up over his shoulder. Thomas appeared in the wheelhouse door and gave him a thumbs-up sign.

He braced himself, and grinned when the *Hari Kiri XIII* suddenly leapt forward, veered hard to port, and no longer paid attention to the rules of the watery road. It made use of its size and an excruciatingly loud air horn to bully its way through the thickening collection of boats, swamping those who weren't large enough, raising angry shouts from those who barely got out of the way with their trim intact.

It was a remarkable feat of nautical skill which he acknowledged with a two-fingered salute toward the bridge, just before he felt his face turn green, his stomach leave its accustomed place below his ribs, and his breakfast make a torturous journey toward his throat.

He barely made it to the head in time.

And when he returned, Molly was standing in the middle of the cabin, hands on her hips and shaking her head.

"I thought you were a sailor."

"Tailor," he corrected, grasping for a chair to collapse in.

"I see."

"Good, because I can't." He passed a hand over his eyes. "God, I think I'm going to die."

"Thomas says we'd better get ready. The captain isn't going to be able to come to a full stop when we get to wherever we're going."

He looked at her, looked away to the water, and looked back. "Swim? We're going to have to swim?"

"Coral reefs," she reminded him; the islands were surrounded by them, and apparently it was far too dangerous bringing a boat of this size in to the place they wanted to go at this speed, unless Linc wanted them to drop anchor and let Pigmeo catch up.

Then she leaned closer. "Hey, can't you swim?"

"Of course, I can swim!" he snapped. "I just prefer to do it in my bathtub, that's all."

With an exasperated glance toward heaven, she double-checked her gun, stuffed extra cartridges into her pockets, and waited for him to join her on deck. He stalled by a return to the head to get rid of dessert. He stalled by splashing cold water over his face. He stalled by peering out to the island and groaning silently when he saw the inhospitable shoreline, the tropical forests beyond, and above them all the menacing, smoking summits of Hawaii's Volcano National Park.

Then Molly grabbed his arm and pulled him above where Thomas was waiting.

The irregular cast of the shore was marked by spits of bare rock that reached into the sea, by gleaming white beaches beyond the underwater pastel fences of coral, and by fences erected by the park service to prevent sightseers from landing where they weren't wanted. Lincoln knew they were heading for a small cove known to Norkuro for reasons he didn't bother to ask; what he didn't know was how far in they would be able to go before they had to leave ship and swim.

He hoped it wasn't more than a few yards.

"Boy," Thomas said anxiously as they rounded a narrow projection of wave-drenched dark rock and the engines cut power swiftly. "You have to leave now."

Molly stood at the railing, checked her gun tucked into her waistband, and turned. "Well?"

Lincoln said, "I don't see anything but a lot of palm trees."

"Lincoln, come on!"

"And what's all that steam back there?"

Thomas looked as the cruiser slowed slightly and the captain shouted an order.

"Lava," the Hawaiian said. "Part of the flow is there."

The swim wasn't as far as it looked, and farther than he would have liked, but once on the shell-and-sand narrow beach, he felt much better. He turned to wave, but the *Hari Kiri XIII* was already vanishing eastward, and Molly was already plowing her way into the forest.

He followed quickly, caught up, and forced her to stop for a moment.

"But we can't waste time!"

"Then tell me which way to go."

She looked around her at the palms, giant ferns, and other growth, and pointed. Then changed her mind and pointed in another direction. And a third. And then at his chest. "So where?"

He could see her face shadowed with anxiety, and he smiled his sympathy, took her hand and led her westward. "This way," he said quietly.

"How did you know this path was here?"

"I didn't. But I figured that the rangers have to get around, and they have to do it fast, and they probably have regular routes. Boy, look at the size of that orchid! I also figure that your brother will probably want to stay close to one of these routes so he can move as fast as we are if he has to. There are a few people who live here, you know, and while I doubt he's made contact with any of them, it wouldn't hurt to ask around."

"You know where they are?"

"I haven't the slightest idea."

"Then . . . then . . ."

The air was filled with the taint of sulphur, and every so often the ground trembled slightly beneath their feet—it was less an actual feeling of movement than a sensation that the earth wasn't as solid as they'd like. Occasional thin clouds of smoke drifted down from the thick foliage, turning the green-tinted air a momentary ugly grey.

The trails made it much easier to climb the rising land, and to stay away from major dirt roads where they heard vehicles driving, perhaps one every fifteen minutes. He suspected they were rangers looking to get people out of the park in case of disaster, or scientists making the rounds of their measuring equipment. In either case, he didn't want to have to explain himself, because an overzealous ranger would have them out of the park on the double, and a scientist would have phone contact with the rangers, who would fetch them out of the park on the double.

Two hours later the trail they were following abruptly widened to a clearing. Three large wood huts were on the far side, their cone-shaped roofs thatched with palm fronds. A rusted and engineless pickup was abandoned between two of them, and when Molly called out a hello before he could stop her, there wasn't a sound in response.

It was hot.

A bird called back in the forest.

Grumblings like muffled explosions drifted down from the cloud-shrouded peaks to their right.

And the smell of burning sulphur was much stronger.

"Now what?" she asked, dropping wearily to the ground. "Hey, it's warm down here!"

He pulled her back up and led her around the huts to the trail's continuation.

"More?"

He nodded.

"Lincoln, where are we going?"

"As close to Kilauea as we can get."

183

She balked. "You're crazy! We'll get fried."

"All right. Then we'll stand on the road up there and wait for him."

"But—"

"Right."

They walked.

And the heat intensified. He knew that unlike the eruptions of Mount St. Helens and the Mediterranean volcanos, Kilauea and its massive crater expended more lava and smoke and the occasional flying boulder than anything else; the lava would spill over the lip or through new and old cracks and follow the paths burned by previous eruptions. He also knew that if Montague Partridge was actually testing the statuette—for which he still clung to a bit of doubt, just for the relief of it—he would not be dispassionate enough to do whatever he had to and then leave to observe at a distance. He would want to stay nearby, in case he was wrong and had to do it again.

Whatever "it" was.

He also knew that Cull and his men had probably already figured that out.

Another two hours, and two more clearings, these deserted park stations for tourists.

The grumblings grew louder.

Perspiration drenched them, matting their hair to their skulls and making them feel as if their boots had been filled with tepid water.

They heard no more birds.

They stumbled upon a badly paved road and found themselves looking down a steep denuded slope into a shallow depression less than a mile away. In its center was a long band of dull black that steamed furiously, and in the black's center a ragged streak of brilliant red and white.

"Lord," Lincoln said.

"Lava," she said. "It cools on the sides."

They looked up, to the split and jagged edge of Kilauea crater almost a full mile across, and saw the glowing exit points through which the lava poured, swiftly at first as it plunged down the sides, then more sluggishly as its outer fringes cooled, and it was pushed from the lava flowing behind.

"Fascinating," he said.

"Scary."

He thought terrifying was a better word, but declined to argue. Instead, they followed the road as far as they could, ducking out of sight into the thick underbrush whenever a small plane flew too close for comfort, neither of them wanting to admit now that they would have to depend on luck to find Molly's brother.

He could be anywhere—on the crater itself, in the forest around it, or Lincoln could have figured him completely wrong and he could be safely on a boat in a cove, watching the display through binoculars.

He didn't want to think about that.

Molly trudged beside him, forcing herself to hurry, scanning both sides of the road as if she could strip away the greenery by sheer will to make the search easier.

They found nothing.

Molly swore loudly, and demanded of the shadows that Monty stop playing games and get his butt out here where she could give it a swift kick.

Twice, by tacit consent, they collapsed on the verge and lay in what shade they could find, gasping for breath in the thick air and mopping the sweat from their faces with their sleeves. He would have killed then for a drink of water, and she could have killed him if he didn't offer her any.

The third time they stopped, he noted that the trees were less high, the ferns almost gone, and the lava seemed to flow more strongly than ever. He wondered if they were planning to evacuate Hilo; he wondered if Pigmeo had ever caught up with Thomas; he wondered as he looked down at the ground who in hell would want to smoke a cigarette in a place like this.

"Hey," he said softly, sitting up and grabbing for the cigarette. "Does Monty smoke?"

"No."

He held the tip close to his face. "Someone does. This thing is still lit."

A footstep sounded behind him.

He looked over his shoulder quickly, but was too late to lift a hand to stop the bearded giant he saw from crashing a boulder down on his head.

NINETEEN

THE SKY HAD TURNED RED.

Or the blow had somehow affected his vision.

When he blinked his eyes open and groaned at the lances that seemed buried in his skull, he could see nothing but a red glow that pulsed unevenly, and could hear nothing but the screaming of a headache that made him close his eyes again.

The pain passed.

When he looked a second time the red was still there, and within seconds his eyes had adjusted.

"I am going to die," he announced hoarsely, "and I'll kill the man who tries to stop me."

He was lying on a bed of grass and fern under a low conical roof raised from the ground on a series of stakes not quite close enough to form a wall. He could hear, outside and amid the grumblings from the volcano, the night birds of the tropical forest attempting to make their presence known. And he could feel the heat—damp and pressing, like cotton saturated with water.

On the ground to his right was a battery-powered lantern softly glowing.

A test of his arms and legs proved he wasn't

bound, but when he tried to raise his head he knew he might as well have been—the ache ordered him sternly to stay prone, don't move, and if you're lucky your head will fall off.

There was a rustling to his left.

He moved his eyes and saw a shadow pass between the roof's rough supports and kneel beside him.

"You didn't tell me," he said accusingly, "that you had an idiot for a brother."

"Oh, Lincoln, you don't know how sorry I am," Molly said, leaning down to kiss his cheek. "He didn't know. He thought you were working for Cull."

He might have commented, but he didn't. He tried to lift himself on his elbows again, and fought off the wave of vertigo that churned his stomach when she put an arm behind his back to help him. That, too, passed, and he sagged forward, his arms draped limply across his thighs. A gourd filled with water was touched to his lips, and he drank greedily, spitting out the first gulp to cleanse his mouth, then swallowing until the gourd was empty and taken away. A moment afterward, a cool, wet cloth was placed on the back of his head, and he winced.

"You've got a bump," she said quietly.

"What I've got is a hole in the head."

"He's sorry."

"He's doomed if I ever recover."

"That's a little harsh, don't you think?"

"Not the way I feel now."

"Besides, he's much bigger than you are."

"I am," he said after a pause, "also known for my charity."

The cloth was replaced with a fresh one, and he held it there himself, blinking, taking deep breaths, and staring directly ahead where he saw the red sky, the glow from the eruption providing a display that was as awesome as it was frightening. The lava flowed gold, white, and crimson, and every so often a puff of white smoke would trail toward the stars.

"It works?" he asked.

Molly nodded. "I'm afraid so."

"And Cull?"

"No sign of him."

A shadow moved between his line of sight and Kilauea, and he leaned away from it as it approached. It was a huge figure that soon resolved itself into a man who could have been Molly's giant twin had it not been for the beard that reached down to the center of his khaki-shirted chest.

"Mr. Blackthorne, what can I say?" Montague Partridge said as he knelt before him.

"Molly explained."

"Still, I hope you'll accept my apologies."

"I do, don't worry about it."

"Well, as long as you do, I won't upset myself over the condition of your cranial covering, though I would hope that in future you will refrain from exposing that covering to dastardly blows such as the one I inflicted upon you whilst you were mesmerized by the display."

Lincoln nodded; he needed no further proof of Montague's identity.

"And now I suppose we'd best get down to business."

Despite Kilauea's position, he could see a gleam of red in the man's eyes. It was, he thought, either a hint of madness, or the man was part deer.

There was something in Partridge's hand.

"Well," the man said cheerfully when he followed Lincoln's gaze, "you've guessed my secret."

The hand moved, and Lincoln saw the Odin Soldier for the first time.

The Soldier was perhaps fourteen inches high and carved from wood. It depicted, as he had seen in Pigmeo's photograph, a Viking warrior standing with legs apart and his hand holding a massive sword over his head. The helmet was horned, the left hand held a banded shield over his chest, and over his left eye was a slightly convex patch. It was curiously light for its size, he noted as he hefted it once, gingerly, but he could not deny that the workmanship was superb, and the time it spent lost in the Norwegian cave had not dulled the detail work which, he saw when he held it close to his eyes, was complete down to the studs on the shield's iron strappings.

Yet despite its ferocious stance, it didn't seem capable of making a volcano blow its molten stack.

He was about to hand it back when he noticed that the patch's lower rim was not part of the carved cheek; a closer look, and he saw the faint dotted indication of a hinge in the center.

His finger moved to pry it up.

Montague yelled.

Molly slapped his hand away.

Lincoln gasped, dropped the statuette and pushed himself back, heedless of the sudden sharp pain at his nape. "What? What'd I do now?"

Then he watched in bewilderment as Montague took a deep breath and picked the Soldier up, carefully holding it around its middle as though it might suddenly duck its head and take a piece from his arm. Linc supposed there was something like a poison needle or other some such contraption there, but changed his mind when Molly nodded and Montague half-turned, held the Soldier out and, with one trembling finger, gently raised the patch.

The ground trembled.

Montague lowered the flap.

Lincoln looked to Kilauea and saw no new activity above the crater's rim.

"Oh Christ," he said.

"Odin, Wotan, Wodin," Partridge said after fetching Lincoln another drink. "His name, depending upon the translation and the literacy of the translator. Wednesday is called after him, and he was the chief of the Norse gods until the Ragnarok, the twilight of the gods, the final curtain, the last hurrah. This little figure here is supposedly one of his warriors emulating him right down to the patch. Odin only had one eye, you see, but it didn't diminish his power.

"Now, we modern-day, civilized dwellers on this planet tend not to believe in gods and goddesses who affect our daily lives in not always logical and sometimes capricious ways. Which is odd, since many of us do believe in the Christian god, the Jewish god, and so forth. The idea, though, of several of them ganging up on us doesn't seem right for the time, I suppose.

"That's why churches are sacred and the Parthenon is a tourist attraction."

"This, however, is going to change all that."

Lincoln nodded thoughtfully. He didn't really follow the man's drift, but as long as he eventually got to the point, he'd be polite and listen . . . while he listened for the sounds of approach through the forest.

"This Soldier, according to the notes—you do know about the notes, Mr. Blackthorne?"

He nodded quickly, not wanting to go through all that again.

"Well, this fellow was supposedly a fixture in Asgard, Odin's home. When the gods fell and, some believed, didn't die at all but became mere mortals, the priests of the religion discovered the artifact, recognized its worth and more than symbolic value, and hid it from the new Christians who were converting people at a furious rate.

"It was lost.

"And now it's found.

"And I've got it. You've seen how it works. The world knows something is going on. And—"

"Quiet," Lincoln said with a chop of his hand. He cocked his head, frowned, and rose stiffly from the bedding to stand at one of the supports. With all the talk, the volcano's belching, and the lava hissing, he wasn't sure, but neither could he say that he didn't hear something moving stealthily out there in the dark, something considerably larger than a bread box and infinitely more dangerous.

When he was satisfied he had been mistaken, he turned and slipped his hands into his pockets. "And what, Monty? Now that you have it, and you've proved it contains a certain amount of impressive power, what the hell are you going to do with it?"

"I'm going to save the world!"

Oh god, he thought.

"See?" Molly said.

"Oh shut up," he told her. "You want to kill Cull."

"Sure, but I want to save the world, too."

He sighed, louder when he saw Montague smiling and nodding enthusiastically. "I probably shouldn't ask, but how are you going to do it?"

"I'll give a demonstration, and demand that the world disarm itself or I'll blow it up."

"Huh?"

"Of course!" Molly said.

"How is that saving the world?" he wanted to know. "It looks to me like six of one, half-dozen of another."

"Only on the surface, Mr. Blackthorne, only on the surface."

Lincoln looked to the volcano; the man had a point.

"On the other hand," he said into the ensuing silence, "Cull would want it to set himself up as a ruler."

"The Emperor Ming of Earth," Molly agreed with a sharp nod.

Another silence, until he broke it again. "Well, now that we've found you, I suppose we'd better get out of here before Cull or one of his boys comes along."

Molly agreed; Montague wanted to stick around and watch the fireworks, but he was overruled and, after nearly fifteen minutes of debate, decided that it would be best, now that he had proven to himself that the Soldier was functional, to find his way to the corridors of power so he could start knocking on some doors.

"You understand, of course," Lincoln told him, "that nobody's going to believe you."

Montague pointed to Kilauea. "That's proof enough."

"Coincidence. That's all they have to say before they lock you away."

Montague was not fazed. "Then I'll knock down a few buildings and punch a few holes in the streets."

"Then don't do it in New York," he said. "They'll never notice the difference."

"I am not a fool, Mr. Blackthorne."

Lincoln never thought he was, and he said so as earnestly as he could; what he didn't give voice to was the suspicion that the man would really do what he threatened—he'd literally pull the earth apart at the seams in order to prevent the superpowers from doing it for him. When he looked to Molly, however, he saw nothing but admiration for her brother's goal, and an eagerness to get on with it.

"Then let's go."

"Where?" she asked.

"Back to the cove. Norkuro's men will keep

checking there until either I send them a message otherwise, or they read our obituaries in the paper."

Partridge readily agreed, and set about putting his things together in a backpack Lincoln thought large enough to hold his own entire wardrobe. When they were ready, Montague looked wistfully at the crater, steadied himself when a tremor rippled through the forest, then jerked his head sideways in a signal to get on.

Lincoln led the way with the lantern. He wasn't afraid of being stopped now. One look at the bearded giant pulling up the rear and any ranger worth his salary and valuing his life would head the other way. What he worried about were the night-sounds mingling in with Kilauea's thunder—they still bothered him, though he couldn't quite put a finger on exactly what it was about them that tickled some vague notion of familiarity.

There was, however, something definitely out of tune, and consequently he spent as much time listening hard to the birds and whatever else was out there as he did watching his footing. At night, and in spite of the lantern, the trail was treacherous, and more than once one of them inadvertently stumbled over a dark root, a half-buried rock, or a depression that snagged an ankle and threatened to sprain it.

The night deepened, but the temperature did not drop.

Small winged things darted around the lantern's face, and often as not, onto his neck and face. He figured that by the time they reached the cove, he'd either be bled dry or would have slapped himself silly.

Molly said nothing to him; she was too busy talking with her brother, scolding him for leading her halfway across the world like this, and trying to refine his plan to contact the leaders they both felt would be the most reasonable, and the most influential. Montague pressed for the President of the United States or the Prime Minister of England; Molly suggested one or two prominent newscasters or the King of Saudi Arabia.

The discussion became an argument.

The argument created a freeze that lasted for the better part of an hour, until they reached the clearing he had encountered first after leaving the *Hari Kiri XIII*.

The three huts and the pickup were still there.

The only thing different was the man who stepped out of the middle hut and shot Lincoln in the chest.

TWENTY

"CROWS," HE MUTTERED.

"What?" Molly asked, her voice distant and slurred.

"Crows."

"What about them?"

"I heard crows in the forest."

"Oh."

"That's why I knew something was wrong."

"Oh."

"Crows," he mumbled, and drifted back to sleep, awakened only a few minutes later and rolled onto his side. He retched hard enough to bring pain to his chest, and knew it was only a reaction to the sedation he had been given in the tranquilizer dart Molahu had shot at him.

Then he realized his legs were tied at the ankles.

When he tried to sit up, he realized his wrists were tied behind him.

The sky was brighter than he remembered it being before he'd been drugged, and he thought it must be dawn.

He was wrong.

When his eyes finally cleared, he saw Molly lying

beside him, tears dried on her face, wet hair in dark strands like webbing across her cheeks. Then he looked around and saw the three huts, the pickup, and from between their walls a high black wall. He stared, looked up, and saw the tops of the trees outlined against the glow of the volcano.

Many of them were burning.

As he watched, one of them began to topple sideways.

Then the black wall split with a crackling, popping sound, and a fresh flow of lava poured sluggishly toward them.

"Molly, get up!" he shouted, rolling over to her and thumping against her.

She stirred, but barely opened her eyes. "Crows?"

"Lava."

"No soap. We're safe."

He kicked at her awkwardly until she yelped and tried to kick back. Then he thrust out his chin and she turned just as the center hut burst into flame.

"Omigod, lava!"

"He knew it all along, the bastard," Lincoln said as he started to roll out of the flow's path. "He knew there'd be a stream of it moving down here, and it's easier to do it this way than dump us in the ocean."

He stopped when his ankles refused to move any farther.

"Lincoln, we're tethered!"

"You're kidding!"

She wasn't; they were.

Two tall stakes had been driven into the ground, the ends of their ropes tied to the bases. The stakes were between them and the lava.

They were as far away from it as they were going to get.

"Well, damn," he said.

Molly backed off until her rope would give no more; then she sat up and gaped as a second hut exploded into flames; sparks drifted lazily into the air.

"I saw a movie once," she said as he wriggled on his back to her side, "where this woman who knew Victor Mature or someone ran in front of some lava to pick up her baby, and they were run over. God, it looked like mud, not like this, and it moved a lot faster."

The cooling sides of the flow snapped loudly when large chunks of lava broke off and rolled into the trees. They were cool enough to harden, but still hot enough to leave tiny fires behind.

Perspiration showered into Lincoln's eyes and he shook his head vigorously to clear them.

The third hut became a torch, and the pickup burned as it was turned by the flow's force onto its side.

"Maybe it'll stop," she said hopefully.

He doubted it; the lava was heading relentlessly for the sea, and there wasn't anything short of a two-day downpour or Pigmeo's singing that was going to stop it in time. He hated himself for it then, but he looked up to pray for a tropical storm, and saw the moon grinning back. He shrugged. Oh well, he thought; nothing ventured, nothing gained. Then he felt the ground trembling, and he gagged at the sulphuric stench when a hot breeze altered direction to blow straight at them.

Hotter, and he didn't want to believe that he felt his clothes beginning to singe; as it was, his sweat was turning to steam when it dropped off his chin and landed on his shirt.

"Your knife!" Molly shouted then over the roar of the moving cauldron. "Use your knife!"

It must be the heat fogging my brain, he thought; he should have thought of that before instead of sitting here like a dummy and admiring the aesthetics of natural destruction.

He leaned as far forward as he could to give his wrists room before flexing his forearm gently. Thus delicately positioned, the knife would then slip carefully out of the sheath instead of being fired out, and with the point caught against the fold of his wrist, he ought to be able to saw through the rope long before the lava reached them.

The knife jammed in his cuff.

"Well?"

"I can't," he said. "It's stuck."

"Oh, great."

He moved forward to give the rope slack, then raised his knees in an attempt to bring his hands under his buttocks and out front where he might be able to use the knife as it was.

Hotter still, and his skin began to redden, to feel as if it were going to peel from his face.

"Lincoln, it's moving faster."

The huts were long gone, smashed into fiery splinters and ash while the pickup had vanished.

His arms weren't long enough.

"My god!" he said angrily.

"Don't you have something in your boots?" she demanded.

"Don't be stupid, of course not."

"Christ, they do in the movies."

He glared at her, glared at the hissing, thundering monster that crawled toward them, and felt his jaw drop.

"What?" she said when she saw his expression.

"The lava," he said.

"What about it?"

"It's going to reach the stakes before it reaches us."

"So what? That means we'll have ten feet left to . . . oh!" She squinted at him, at the stakes, and grinned. "Boy, is Cull dumb."

"Assuming we don't fry first."

And there was nothing to do but wait, to watch as a bird watches a cobra as the lava spread out in the clearing, rumbling still and popping sparks and globes of molten rock into the air. A tree to their right sputtered into flame; one to their left was pushed over as the flow burned away the lower portion of its fibrous trunk.

Lincoln rolled onto his stomach and shoulder-crawled until the rope was taut, instructing Molly to do the same and keep her eyes closed in hopes of preventing them from drying out. The soles of his boots warmed. Grew hot. Grew so hot he could feel the soles of his feet tightening and readying to sprout blisters. Every few seconds, when he wasn't overcome by the enervating temperature, he pulled at the rope, hard and swift.

"I'm scared," Molly said, her voice cracking.

He yanked again, something inside trying to fool him into believing the rope was stretching.

"They took Monty."

And with Monty, the Soldier.

He tugged, and was sure now—the rope was beginning to fray. He looked over his shoulder, then, and saw his stake curled about with serpentine blue flame.

A fat stream of lava flowed swiftly toward them. The rope held.

Molly grunted, rolling onto her back and thrashing about on the ground, trying to help the fire, trying to avoid the fire-river that was less than a yard from her feet.

"It's not fair," she gasped. "You're taller than I am."

He pulled, the tendons on his neck red and swollen, his lungs filled with searing air and holding, his hips protesting the strain, his ankles feeling as if they were going to leave their sockets.

Then Molly shrieked, whirled, and scrambled to her knees.

"Hot damn!" she said, crawled to Lincoln, took hold of the rope and pulled, swearing, blaspheming, casting oaths upon Cull and his minions that would have turned his white hair black had he heard them.

His feet burned, and he could feel the skin cracking.

Molly slapped his legs in frustration, and he rolled away from her angrily, just enough to pull his legs free as the stake fell and the lava rushed forward.

* * *

He didn't know how they did it, but they ran. Plunging away from the clearing into the forest, down the slope in the hellishly red dark, falling more than once and not feeling a thing, careening off boles and boulders and not caring because the air was so much cooler, the hissing dimmer and, through a break in the giant ferns, they could see glimpses of the sea.

There wasn't another inch in his legs, another step in his feet, but he kept on, for a hundred yards holding Molly's waist to keep her from falling, for another hundred yards their positions reversed.

And when they fell out of the forest onto the beach, they didn't even have the strength to laugh at their good fortune.

Nor were they able to do much more than yell weakly when they saw the darkened form of the *Hari Kiri XIII* waiting on the other side of the reef. For the moment they didn't care if anyone heard them; for the moment they only cared that there was water ahead, and as soon as they found the wherewithal they were going to crawl there and get so goddamned wet not even Kilauea herself would be able to touch them.

The launch came five minutes later, and Thomas and two crew members carried them aboard, motored them out to the boat and laid them in staterooms. Their clothes were removed, their bodies bathed, and before any of it was finished they were both asleep from exhaustion.

Sometime shortly after dawn he awoke.

The cruiser wasn't moving, but a look out the

porthole and he knew they had sailed to another cove; from the position of the sun he knew they were on the other side of the island. He felt as bad as he had in years, but considering the alternative he had no right to complain, which he didn't as he swung out of his bunk, and his legs gave way, and he dropped to the floor.

A minute later he was staggering up to the deck. Molly was in one of the canvas chairs, drinking a large glass of orange juice and scanning the horizon through a pair of binoculars. She turned when she saw him, smiled brightly, and waved to Thomas, who was standing at the wheelhouse door. The young man vanished, and reappeared with a tray of glasses as Lincoln fell into the chair beside her.

"You look all right," he said, taking two glasses from Thomas and gesturing the tray to the deck between them.

"I'll live," she said, grinning.

Thomas waited.

Lincoln sighed. "Now what."

"The captain respectfully wishes to know where we are going, Mr. Blackthorne."

"Honolulu," Molly said instantly.

"No," Lincoln said.

"Why not?"

"Cull has your brother."

"I know. And he has the Soldier. There isn't anything we can do now but get back to Honolulu, notify the authorities and get the Coast Guard or the Navy or something out here to find them."

"They're not here."

She started to ask, then changed her mind. "Oh."

"Right."

"Wow," Thomas said nervously.

"Tell the captain to go where he has to, to refuel. Then he's going to take us to Kampollea. And if he refuses," he added when Thomas made to protest, "he can leave the boat to us and we'll go. I'm sure Mr. Norkuro will understand."

"Oh boy," Thomas said with a shake of his head, and walked very slowly back to the bridge. It didn't take long for them to hear the captain's high-pitched complaints, which went on for what seemed like an hour before Thomas returned, glum and gnawing on his lower lip.

"The captain says he will take you partway. You can use the motor launch the rest of the way."

"Fair enough," Lincoln said, as he put the glass against his forehead and reveled in the chill. Then he closed his eyes and dozed, ignoring Molly's apprehensive questions by feigning deeper sleep, which indicated quite strongly complete control of the situation.

I am an idiot, he thought.

And thought it again an hour later when the *Hari Kiri XIII* completed its refueling and headed west, out to sea.

"How long?" he asked Thomas at one point.

"I am to tell you when we have an hour to go before we drop you off."

"Good. And how long does the captain estimate it will take us to get to the island?"

"Forever," said Thomas.

Lincoln glowered at him and retired to the main cabin. There he pulled up his sleeve and checked the working of the knife sheath and its spring, wondering what had gone wrong and why he depended on nonsense like this. He wasn't a violent man anyway, and much preferred round table discussions to busting his knuckles on some stranger's chin. Not to mention vice-versa.

Molly stayed away.

Thomas soon joined him and suggested they check the launch for supplies both mechanical and medicinal. He was about to agree when Molly flew into the room, waving the binoculars.

"We're being followed!" she declared breathlessly.

"You've said that already," he reminded her.

"I don't care. We're being followed, and that shrimp is still singing."

Lincoln rushed past her to the companionway, climbed the stairs and had just time enough to see Pigmeo wave at him before the deck exploded.

TWENTY-ONE

THE BLAST SAILED FLAMING DEBRIS OVER HIS HEAD
as he dropped to the steps and yanked Molly down
beside him. His ears buzzed, his eyes stung, and his
head felt as if it had been shoved into a vise. The
smoke was thick and acrid, but was quickly dispersed by the wind created by the cruiser's swift
retreat, and when he looked up again he saw a gaping, smoldering hole just this side of the bow rail,
where the deck chairs and table used to be.

And even as he watched, the hole incredibly grew
larger as the wood slowly began to split along invisible fault lines.

Squinting, then, against the sun's glare and the
tears caused by the smoke, he saw Pigmeo's yacht a
hundred yards back. Arturo was standing beside
the deck gun with binoculars trained on the *Hari
Kiri XIII*, and another man, the gunner, stood behind a tall, split steel shield that reached to his chin.

Lincoln still had no idea what sort of gun it was,
and quickly lost interest in its specifications when it
fired again, the cruiser hove left, and a geyser lifted
from the sea to shower them with warm water.

"Damnit, Lincoln, I thought they were supposed

to fire a warning shot across your bow before they attacked," Molly complained when he pushed her aside and ran front again. "This is piracy, isn't it?"

"Only if they board us and torture the women and children," he answered, knowing how foolish he looked with a puny revolver in his hand against something that was large enough to methodically blow them out of the water. But it made him feel better and he held on to it when he crouched at deck level and peered around the rise of the bridge. He could hear, above in the wheelhouse, the captain shouting hoarse orders into the intercom, and below he could hear the multilingual panicked curses of a number of men. There was the crack of a rifle, another shot from the cruiser chasing them, and another geyser, this one closer, only a few yards shy to port.

Molly knelt beside him, nervously tapping the barrel of her gun on her thigh. "They ought to correct for windage."

He glared at her, then grabbed a safety rail when the captain swung the cruiser starboard again, then port, barely missing a pair of shots that flanked them directly behind.

The rifle fired again.

The trailing yacht closed.

A doorway opened in the side, and a handful of crewmen fell out on deck, turning to the captain and screaming at him in languages Linc didn't understand. The captain shoved aside one of the windows and screamed back. The crew shook its collective head. The captain pointed disgustedly, the men ran to the stern, and less than two minutes later

Lincoln, unbelieving, saw them crowded in the motor launch, frantically putting distance between themselves and the yacht.

"Rats," Molly said with a sneer.

The second cruiser closed, fifty yards now, and Lincoln made his way along the narrow passage until he was even with the superstructure's rear wall.

Arturo leaned forward, lowered the binoculars and waved.

"Well, damn," said Lincoln, raised his arm and fired.

Arturo's binoculars split in half.

The cannon roared again.

Another hole exploded in the deck.

And before Linc could lift himself up, a shell landed squarely atop the bridge. The wheelhouse windows blew out, the *Hari Kiri XIII* shuddered, and he found himself sliding inexorably toward the sea as the deck canted sharply. He barely managed to grab a slick brass post, had to abandon his revolver to use his other hand and shouted for Molly when he saw the racing, bubbling water less than five feet beneath him.

She didn't answer.

The cruiser shuddered at a muffled explosion belowdecks.

Pigmeo's boat fired again, and a shell shattered the prow and flung Lincoln side to side, slamming him into the hull.

His right hand slipped off.

Smoke poured from the portholes to either side of him and blinded him, made him gag, and filled his eyes with tears.

The yacht raced on, noticeably lower in the water.

He reached for the post with his right hand, found it, and held on, linking his fingers and feeling his arms threatening to pull away from his shoulders. He dangled there for a moment, too engrossed in his imminent demise to think; then with a grunt he swung one leg up and over the edge of the deck, balanced there for several seconds, and yelled as he threw himself under the railing and rolled to the wall.

The smoke cleared in a gust of wind, and he was able to see Pigmeo's boat swinging rapidly away. Then the smoke closed again, and all he could see was the tattered sleeves of his shirt, and all he could hear was the sound of his own ragged breathing.

A gap appeared in the deck not three feet from his face, and a gout of flame burst into the air. He scrambled backward, averting his face but keeping as close to the cabin wall as he could. When he reached the foredeck, he flung himself around the corner and swore when the cruiser listed again to port, heavily, almost too rapidly for him to snare the open companionway frame.

He hauled himself up until he could look down the stairwell, and he groaned—the cabin was filling with oil-slick water, sticks and frames of furniture bobbed on the surface, and thick curls of smoke carried with them the distinct odor of fire.

There was no sense attempting to climb down now; if Molly was there, she was dead. So he continued to move upward, grabbing at anything he thought would hold him back from the ocean that now began to wash over the side.

His arms ordered him to knock it off; his head, though clear now, ordered him to get a rest; and his chest, scraping along the hot, splintered deck, cautioned him about the loss of blood and his heart rate.

The engines died, a violent tremor raced through the boat, and he heard the unmistakable sounds of the hull breaking up.

The *Hari Kiri XIII* slowed, and stopped.

The deck canted at a sharper angle, making his climb almost vertical now; or, he thought, he could just wait a few minutes and let the boat sink to his level.

Fire spouted briefly out of the companionway hatch, scorching his soles and sending him scrambling again, this time to the starboard railing, which he used to pull himself upright.

Wood groaned, steel buckled, and glass popped and cracked. The rail was almost too hot to hold onto, but he moved cautiously aft, searching for signs of Molly, trying to peer through the smoke-clogged portholes, behind and ahead of him at the same time. He kept telling himself he had a few minutes more, but when the stern gurgled under the low rolling waves, he knew he had to get off and fast or he was going to be sucked down with the boat when it finally gave up the ghost.

He was too late.

With a chorus of eerie, inhuman screams Sol Norkuro's yacht suddenly fell apart as if it had been constructed out of matchsticks and glue, and Lincoln was tossed headfirst into the Pacific Ocean.

Well, hell, I'm going to die, he thought as he kicked frantically toward the surface; and I didn't even have time to make my own burial suit. The idea galled him, and his kicks became stronger, his lungs emptied more rapidly, and when his face finally broke into the air, he gasped so loudly he startled himself.

"Now I know what all those cracks were for. Pretty clever, if I do say so myself."

He shook his head vigorously to clear his eyes, treaded water as best he could, and saw Molly floating toward him on what looked like a raft made for fastidious preppies who didn't want to get their feet wet. It was ungainly in its riding three feet above the swells, and it couldn't have been more than five feet on an irregular side. But if it was good enough to hold her, it was good enough for him.

Besides, the last time he had kicked his right leg he had struck something, and he knew damned well he wasn't tall enough to reach bottom.

Molly took his outstretched hand and pulled him up, laid him out on his stomach and knelt astride him, her hands in the middle of his back, her weight alternately pushing and releasing him until he protested.

"I'm getting the water out of your lungs," she scolded.

"Thank you," he gasped, "but I'm all right."

"You don't look all right," she said sourly. "You look like you went down with the ship."

"I did."

She shrugged and sat beside him.

He closed his eyes in relief, hoping that the next time he opened them he would be back in New Jersey, having the time of his life stabbing himself with his needles.

"I think we're in trouble."

He sat up quickly. "Why? Is that little bastard still around?"

"Oh no, he's long gone, thank heavens. I mean *that,*" and she pointed at the ocean with its rhythmic low swells. "And *that,*" and she pointed to a sun that was a flaring white in a pale blue sky. "And *this,*" she added for good measure, thumping the breakaway deck with a fist, indicating that while it was certainly seaworthy, it was a pity Norkuro hadn't had the foresight to add a small compartment to it to hold such things as food and fresh water and signal flares.

"We are," she concluded gloomily, "up the largest creek in the world."

He tended to agree, though he wouldn't admit it. What he needed from her now was a clear head, a dollop of optimism, and a minor though effective traveling spell that would get them the hell out of here.

"I guess," he said with a wry smile, "we're going to have to come up with a plan."

"All right, you gather the wood and I'll build the signal fire."

"Can't you do any better than that?"

She smiled without humor. "I'm taking lessons from an expert in his field."

"For god's sake, Molly, I'm not perfect, y'know."

"I noticed."

"Just give me time to think. I'll come up with something."

"Good," she said. "I'll count the seconds."

A two-foot wooden post protruded from the center of the deck; what it had been before he didn't know, but he used it now to anchor himself while he stood, as if the added height would show him something miraculous he hadn't seen while he had been lounging on his back.

It didn't.

All he had was a clearer view of the water which, under other circumstances, might have been awe-inspiring, breathtaking, and something far beyond the reach of ordinary mortals.

As it was, it was terrifying.

He sat again, one foot hooked around the post, Molly's left foot hooked over his.

The heat, despite the wind that leapt from the tops of the waves, bent their backs and lowered their heads.

Molly wept for almost fifteen minutes.

Lincoln wondered if he could take off his shirt and hers and rig themselves some sort of sail; unfortunately, a two-foot mast wouldn't do them much good unless the wind picked up. Maybe, he thought, he could pry up some planking and somehow fasten it to the post with his trousers and socks. That would only leave them with three or four feet of sitting space, but it was better than nothing.

On the other hand, that might, somehow, do damage to the deck portion's floating ability.

He decided that in the long and short runs it wasn't worth the risk, especially after he examined the raft more closely and realized that short of a crowbar or another sneak assault from the unreliable Pigmeo, they weren't even going to raise a splinter on their behalf.

The raft shook then, and Molly whimpered as she lunged across the post and grabbed him around the waist. He looked down at her back, looked around the immediate vicinity and saw nothing they could have collided with. What he did see, however, was that the wind had changed and they were, as far as he could tell, being pushed farther away from the islands.

So much, he thought, for washing up on shore.

Then Molly smiled sheepishly and straightened. "I'm sorry," she said, wiping her face and eyes with the backs of her hands. "I should be brave, I suppose."

"No need. You're right. We're in trouble."

"Do you think we're going to die?"

The raft shook again, and he had the distinct impression it was about to break apart.

"Maybe."

She shaded her eyes with both hands and looked around them, dropped her arms, and sighed. "We're going west, aren't we."

He nodded.

"There isn't anything out there."

"Unfortunately, there is."

She slumped again, then glared when the raft trembled a third time. "Goddamnit, what the hell's going on?"

"Well," he said calmly after examining the empty ocean, "it's either a remarkable device Sol's hidden in this thing that's trying to give us power, or it's sharks."

"Sharks?"

"I vote for the device. Norkuro, as you've already noted, is a very clever man."

"You lose," she said flatly, and pointed to the dozen or more dark fins that suddenly broke the surface twenty yards away and headed straight for them.

Feeling a bit giddy, he said, "Maybe they're dolphins who are going to push us to the nearest beach."

"Are you kidding? Do you know where the nearest beach is?"

"Unfortunately, yes."

She stared at him, at the fins that were gathering at the rear of the raft, then followed his gaze west, to a narrow dark cloud that rose abruptly out of the water.

"Oh lord, rain?"

"Don't I wish."

The raft trembled slightly yet again, and they eventually felt themselves moving much faster than the wind and currents could account for.

"Lincoln, they're not sharks." She giggled. "My god, you were right."

He shrugged. He'd heard of more outlandish things in his life. Such as being propelled by a school of well-meaning dolphins toward an island where he knew he would probably die.

TWENTY-TWO

KAMPOLLEA HAD A VOICE—A DEEP-THROATED, CON-
tinuous numbing thunder as the surf smashed
ceaselessly against the base of its sheer, inhospitable cliffs, against the high jagged rocks that rose out
of the sea around its shore, against the rocky
beaches that seemed to begin and end nowhere.

It was a spectacular if somewhat dismaying display of sound and millennial destruction, but Lincoln refused to permit himself appreciation of it,
however existential. The moment he touched reasonably dry land and knew he wasn't going to
drown, he headed for a crack in the water-slick
wall, Molly following reluctantly and lightly
touched with doubt. The dolphins were long gone,
deserting their stations just outside a coral reef
when the breakaway deck finally fell apart under
their friendly battering. The subsequent swimming
wasn't as bad as the arriving with the knowledge
that unless they found a way inland soon the tide
was going to sweep them under.

The crack he had seen just before he hit the water
was less than four feet wide, and ended ten feet in.
Molly followed closely as he edged sideways

through the gap and, words useless over the roar of the waves and the cry of the startled seabirds wheeling about the cliff-face, pointed at small indentations in the rock, then pointed upward, toward the darkening sky a thousand feet up. She shook her head. He grinned, nodded encouragement, and started climbing. He hoped she would follow because once he was more than his own height above the ground he had no intention of looking down.

Which he didn't.

Not until he reached a dry, dusty ledge thirty feet up and had scrambled onto it. He panted. He grinned foolishly. He thanked a few gods that he had neither the breath nor the brains to scream, then grabbed Molly's wrists as she appeared over the edge. A single pull had her sitting beside him, and a pointing finger showed her the cave.

She put her lips to his ear: "It's ugly. Does it go all the way through?"

He nodded.

"You've been here before."

He nodded a second time, and moved on before she had a chance to ask about the circumstances. As it was, he could not shake off the chill that walked his spine and settled in his bowels, could not stop himself from thinking about the smoking lake he knew he was going to see in less than an hour.

The cave was not completely dark; from behind it was lit from the funnel of light drifting down from the island's top, and in front there was a large opening filled with a soft white glow. The walls were smooth, the floor littered with broken shells and the scattered bones of birds and small animals, picked clean and sucked free of their marrow. They couldn't see the top; it was buried in a blackness not even the light could penetrate.

When they were halfway in, the surf became muffled and they couldn't hear the birds; the glow dimmed as the moon sank below the level of the peaks.

Fifteen minutes later they stepped into a forest that nearly buried the entrance.

It was too dark to see anything clearly, and after a quick look around to be sure they weren't being waited for, he returned to the cave mouth and sat with his back against the cool rock.

"Now what?" Molly said, settling beside him.

"Now we sleep, wait until morning, and go get your brother."

"When do we kill Cull?"

Only in your dreams, my love, he thought.

"First your brother, then the Soldier, then we try to get out of here."

"What about Cull?"

He closed his eyes, intending only to keep her quiet, but the brunt of exhaustion finally overwhelmed him and he fell asleep, not feeling Molly put her head on his shoulder and do the same.

The dreams were vivid.

He nearly woke twice, groaning and straining, but each time he approached the brink, he drifted off again, back into the nightmares, back into the smoking lake where he struggled futilely on a platform anchored to the lake bed, chained and attempting to escape from something that surged and whirled and moaned just below the roiling surface.

He never saw it.

And it never reached him.

But it was too close, and too big, and too powerful not to have him whimpering for another way, a simpler way to die.

The plane woke him just after dawn.

"The first thing we have to do," he said as they hurried through the forest of ferns, palms, and trees whose boles were a bright and smooth green, "is find out where he's keeping Monty. Then we'll figure out what to do about it."

Molly grunted absently, but she kept looking up through the interlaced foliage. The seaplane's arrival had startled her until he told her about the lake in the island's center, and when it circled several times she had decided they knew she was here and were looking for her.

That he argued with, assuming quite logically that Pigmeo had more than likely radioed his naval success back to Kampollea. With the *Hari Kiri XIII* sunk and all vital hands lost, there was no possible way Montague Partridge could be rescued short of an ambitious amphibious assault by a battalion of crack marines who didn't have anything better to do than climb precipitous cliffs covered with guano.

Unless, of course, someone had spotted the wreckage of the raft, which might well have been driven to the shore by the currents and the waves. Not to mention the dolphins, who may have figured Lincoln would need the debris for firewood.

He sniffed, rubbed the back of his neck, and

wished it were at least twenty degrees cooler, down to about one hundred. As it was, the air was stifling, only the tops of the trees and ferns receiving the benefits of the wind that slipped down the steep slopes.

An hour later Molly asked him if they were lost.

"Not likely. All we have to do is go downhill and we'll hit the lake."

"Good." She wiped her face with a sleeve. "I could use a drink about now."

"I wouldn't drink it if I were you."

"Why?"

He didn't have to explain. They thrashed through a thicket and found themselves on the shore.

"Oh," she said.

"Yeah."

The lake was as circular as the island, and took up all the land not covered by the forest. The wind blew across it to raise small waves, there were tiny clumps of reedlike plants floating about its surface, and here and there, close to shore and in the center, tendrils of pale smoke rose from bubbles that rose to the top and broke slowly, without a sound. Molly knelt and stuck a finger in it.

"It's almost hot," she said in amazement. She put the finger to her tongue and spat quickly. "God, it tastes like my cooking."

"Sulphur," he said, "and a few other things."

Her nose wrinkled. "It smells like . . . like—"

"Kilauea," he provided quickly, lest she was tempted to wax scatological. "You're right. Somewhere under all this is what they call a dead volcano. The trouble with dead volcanos is, they don't know it."

She rose, puffed her cheeks and blew out a slow breath. A hand shaded her eyes as she examined the breadth of the lake and the height of the slopes surrounding it.

"So now I guess we follow the shoreline to Cull's encampment, get my brother, and get out again."

"That's the plan."

"What if it doesn't work?"

"Then we'll find out what Cull had in store for the Soldier."

"He wants to create his own country," a husky voice said behind them.

Molly whirled, hands into fists and ready to fight. Lincoln turned slowly, resigned, and wondering how Cull had found them. He was also getting a little tired of people creeping up on his blind side.

"Well, I'll be," he said with a slow-growing smile.

Molly only squealed in delighted relief and threw her arms around Angel Lymington, hugging him until his face turned red. The aging pilot, now wearing a sharply creased khaki bush jacket, pith helmet, and a sidearm, gently disengaged her and brought them back into the protection of the forest. There they found a log lying athwart a half-hidden path and sat while Lymington explained that he had left the motel as abruptly as he had because he had a duty to his employer, Montague, and he didn't think his two new companions were really up to the arduous task. He had tried to reach Hawaii first, but he couldn't get any of Cull's private aircraft to work. Then he accidentally came across a hunting Takana, who didn't forgive and forget, and had spent the rest of the day hiding in Waikiki, pretending he was an Australian surfer who had lost his way.

"But how did you get here?" Molly asked.

"Cull has two seaplanes. It's how he flies in and out of here with his supplies and his diversions. He took one. I took the other."

It was hidden only a few hundred yards from where they sat, and he figured on breaking Montague out, reaching the plane, and taking off for the safety of the islands.

Lincoln asked if there was much air traffic around here.

Lymington said no.

Lincoln asked if Cull was already on the island.

Lymington, after hesitating, said yes.

Lincoln said nothing.

Lymington smoothed a palm down over his bush jacket, took off his pith helmet and scratched his head ruefully. "I do believe, Mr. Blackthorne, you are trying to tell me that they have unquestionably heard my stealthy approach and are, even now, wondering what I am doing here since I have been, in the recent past, somewhat of a traitor to their cause."

"You could say that."

"Oh, Angel," Molly said.

Lymington replaced the pith helmet, touched the revolver holstered at his side and said, "Then I suppose we had best carry on before we are interfered with."

Lincoln put a hand to his mouth, stared at the ground, and thought furiously for several minutes. When he was finished, he rose, brushed himself off and asked Lymington to lead the way to the encampment. A disturbing memory told him they were only a mile or so away, an hour's cautious trip to the middle of the lake's northern shore.

The pilot agreed and headed off into the brush, following the meandering path with Molly behind and Lincoln trailing, half expecting Cheetah to drop a coconut on his head. They made little attempt to conceal the considerable noise of their passage, believing that Cull would have kept his men close to home and close to Partridge; there was too much forest here to get lost in, too many ways for someone to outflank even the most determined search party and move in from behind.

It wasn't yet noon, but the temperature continued to rise steadily and the activity in the lake increased accordingly.

An hour or so passed before Lymington led them upward in a wide arc that brought them to the middle of the slope and an outcropping of volcanic rock. They lay on it and peered through the tops of the trees below.

"It's ugly," Molly said.

"It serves," Lymington told her.

Lincoln made a sound, a cross between a grunt and a groan.

There were four buildings below them in a wide clearing, each at least thirty feet on a side. All were raised on thick wooden pilings ten feet high, all had stout log walls and were thatched with palm fronds and wide, dark green leaves, and all had fixed ladders at the corners which led from the ground to a narrow porch encircling each structure.

The first was situated directly over the lake itself, its front supports partially submerged and a seaplane tied to a dock that slanted downward and to the left from the porch. The other three ranged in a row behind it; the one on the left had no visible windows.

"I suggest," Lymington whispered behind a hand, "that we wait until nightfall before we begin our assault."

"Great," Molly said eagerly, scrubbing her hands dryly.

"Assault?" Lincoln said. "Who said anything about an assault? This is a rescue mission, not an invasion."

"Do you intend instead to use stealth?"

"How else? You want to swing down like Tarzan and yodel them to death?"

"It is not done that way, Mr. Blackthorne. Full speed ahead, and blacken the whites of their eyes."

"Do you have guns for us?"

Lymington gaped at him, astonished. "You mean you've reached this place without bringing arms with you?"

"Sure."

"Incredible. Incredible!"

"Well," Molly said, "it's really not all that incredible when you look at it. First we had to get away from the boat, then we had to get away from the lava, then we had—"

Lincoln stared her into silence, then shifted to

look down at Cull's hideaway again. He supposed they were keeping Montague in the windowless cabin, and if he was right they would have to get in and out from the front. Which meant exposing themselves to whatever guards were on duty. Which meant there might be a ruckus that would alert Cull and whoever else was there. Which meant the pilot's unuttered but obvious forecast of doom was going to be rather close to the mark.

At best, the odds were even; at worst, they were going to have a hell of a time pulling it off.

But at least, he thought, they would be able to use the seaplane to get away in, as long as Lymington didn't get himself killed, wounded, or otherwise incapacitated.

The ground rocked gently.

"Uh-oh," Molly said.

The center of the lake began to rise as though a monstrous boulder were being raised from beneath, and smoke wafted upward, momentarily hazing the air over the water.

"Amazing," Lymington whispered.

The surface settled again, but left behind it the smoke and a thousand small bubbles that floated for several seconds before beginning to burst.

"I think," Lincoln said, "we'd better not wait until dark."

"Good thinking," said Florenz Cull. "You'd miss dinner, otherwise."

TWENTY-THREE

"Let me ask you something," Lincoln said since there was nothing else he could do, being tied up as he was in the windowless cabin with Molly, Lymington, and Montague, who was in the far corner, unconscious and battered. "Unless, of course, you'd rather just hang around until Cull gets back."

Molly glared at him.

"What the hell were you doing in Maine?"

"Why do you want to know?" she asked sullenly.

"Because I would like to know if all this is mere rotten coincidence, something I said, or if there is the heavy hand of Fate involved."

"If by Fate you mean your friends in New Jersey, then yes."

"Damn."

"They're nice people."

"They have big mouths."

"They didn't want you to stagnate."

Had he been able, then, he probably would have hit her. As it was he was standing against the lefthand wall, his arms over his head and his wrists shackled. Molly was on the opposite wall. Lymington was next to Montague, cocooned in rope and snoring.

She saw where he was looking and shook her head. "Don't blame him. He needs to preserve his energy."

A shadow appeared in the doorless entrance then, and he stiffened. The face was hidden, but the red patch was clear, as was the tiger-headed walking stick in the man's red-gloved hand.

"Welcome back," Cull said as he strode into the room.

"I'm going to kill you!" Molly shouted.

Cull put his back to her, and she berated him for his rudeness.

"Mr. Blackthorne," he said, "we have unfinished business."

"What," Lincoln said. "Me, or your new country?"

"Ah, so you've learned about that, have you?"

"Only rumors."

"Not rumors, Mr. Blackthorne. Fact. With Montague's little man I am going to have a place all my own. A large place. A very large place."

"Which country are you going to destroy to get it?" he said.

"None."

"Look, Florrie, I—" He stopped, did swift mental arithmetic, and didn't believe it.

He looked at Cull.

He believed it.

The man was actually going to attempt to create land the way it had been created in the beginning— with volcanos. He was going to resurrect a few, make himself some new ones, and use the surface thus raised from the sea for his own private empire, maybe even have his own stamps.

"You're crazy."

Cull cocked his head to one side. "I have foresight."

"You only have one eye."

"Is that a crack?"

"It means that you'll probably destroy half the world doing this. The tidal waves will wipe out most of the coastal cities, the earthquakes will split continents . . ." He gasped at the enormity of it. "Jesus, you're out of your mind!"

"I am prepared to make sacrifices."

"Go jump in the lake!" Molly screamed.

Cull looked over his shoulder. "No, my dear. Ladies first."

At that, Molahu and Takana walked in, their civilian clothes exchanged for Hawaiian lava-lava. It would have been laughable had not the muscles that ribbed and ridged their chests and arms been so unpleasantly impressive, and it would have been anachronistic had it not been for the bow and arrows Molahu carried, and the oversized machete Takana tapped against his palm.

Lymington moaned in his chest.

Montague began to shift, and Takana strode over to him, grabbed an arm and yanked him to his feet. Though he was a full head shorter than Partridge, he had no trouble forcing him back across the room toward the door.

"Monty!" Molly called.

Montague stopped and looked at her dazedly.

"Monty, for god's sake, don't let him do it!"

"I am going to have my own island," her brother said through a picket fence of broken teeth. "I have seen the light." Then he shook off Takana's hand and walked out, his guard following with a glance to Cull.

"Crazy as a loon," Molly said glumly. "Just like Father."

Cull laughed shortly and walked over to her, fingered a large key from his shirt pocket and, with Molahu standing watchfully beside him, opened the shackles. She lowered her arms painfully and rubbed at her wrists, then swung her left hand in a roundhouse blow that was, just shy of Cull's right cheek, trapped in Molahu's grip. She struggled. Molahu tightened. She whimpered and sagged, and Molahu took her out.

"It's just you and me now, my friend," Cull said, turning slowly. "Just you and me."

He raised the walking stick and swung it back and forth in front of him, the head cutting the air like a whip, the teeth catching the light and glinting like razors.

Lincoln sucked in his stomach when the head breezed past his middle.

Cull grinned and held up his gloved hand. "Tit for tat, Mr. Blackthorne."

"I'll never sew again."

"You shan't do much else, either, I guarantee it."

The head passed his chest again, and the fabric parted with a hiss that matched the noise he made when he felt the skin below his breast part.

"You might as well relax, Mr. Blackthorne. It's going to take a long, long time."

The room was strangely silent, and Linc couldn't understand why he heard nothing but the passage of the tiger's head. There was something missing, something important, and this time he didn't think it was the out-of-place sound of a crow calling in the forest.

His thighs twitched when the teeth took a piece of his trousers just above the knee.

Outside, he could hear Molly screaming unintelligibly, but he knew it had nothing to do with the way the cabin rocked when the ground shook again.

"Nothing to worry about," said Cull, his face gleaming with perspiration, his one eye opened wide in pleasure. "Just a brief test, that's all. I wouldn't do anything drastic while I was here, would I?"

The tiger sparked over his head, and he ducked instinctively, groaning when he nearly pulled his arms out of their sockets. Then Cull stood less than a foot from him, glaring, baring his teeth and licking his lips. There was the smell of arrogance about him, and madness, and Lincoln could not decide whether to close his eyes and wait, or face it like a man and see death coming.

He closed his eyes.

He heard Cull groan.

He opened them again, and saw the man crumple to the floor.

Lymington instantly grabbed the key and proceeded one-handed to part Linc's shackles. His left hand he held against his chest, stinging from its use as a club.

"He shan't be out for long," the pilot said as the

chains rattled to the floor. "I'm not as strong as I used to be."

Linc was about to tell him it was all right, nothing to worry about, when Lymington yelped and fell into him. Linc pushed him aside just as Cull, from his knees, swung the cane again at the middle of the old man's back.

Linc used his boot and caught Cull on the shoulder, leapt for him and pinned his right hand and the walking stick to the floor while his free hand smacked him on the side of the face. Cull groaned. Linc chopped his throat and rolled off, snatching up the walking stick and waiting as Cull staggered to one knee, gagging and holding his neck.

"Angel, get out," he ordered.

"Sir, he's much too big for you."

"Angel, get the hell out."

Lymington pushed himself to his feet, took one look at Linc's expression and left.

And staggered back in when Molahu punched him full in the chest.

"Get him," Cull rasped, still unable to get to his feet.

Molahu eyed Linc and the tiger-head warily, but advanced, tossing his bow and arrow aside with a sneer of disdain and holding his arms out as if to hug Linc to death.

Linc backed up, kicking Cull's side to topple him out of the way. As Molahu followed, he showed him the tiger's teeth with a pass that only made the Hawaiian show his own teeth in a humorless grin. He swung the deadly weapon and jumped to his right, forcing Molahu to follow at an angle, thinking that he might be able to get to the door and run out, catching the man on the narrow confines of the porch.

Molahu looked behind him at the entrance, raised his arms over his head, and bellowed wordlessly.

"Jesus," Linc said, and swung the stick again.

Molahu brought down his arms and snapped it in half.

"Jesus," Linc said, and dove for the tiger, was caught in midair and gathered to Molahu's chest. He put the heel of his hand under the man's chin and pushed; Molahu tightened his grip. He slapped the man's ears as hard as he could with an open palm; Molahu tightened his grip. He brought his knee up into the man's groin, and Molahu tightened his grip, then yelled and fell backward. Linc pushed out of the embrace, snatched up the tiger and waited, kicking Cull in the side again to keep him from getting up.

Molahu straightened, and charged.

Linc dodged and swung his arm.

Molahu slammed against the rear wall, pivoted and held his hands to his throat in an attempt to stem the rush of blood that spilled over his chest. He fell without a sound.

Lincoln blinked away the sight and headed for the door, stopping only long enough to kick Cull in the side and topple him again. The one eye glared, glazed, and closed.

"It's about time," he muttered, and pressed himself against the frame. A moment to catch his breath, and he looked out, but saw nothing. A check to make sure Cull was still unconscious, a fast count to ten, and he raced along the wobbly porch to the nearest ladder, took it down barely touching the rungs and sprinted to the vanguard building, coming up against the corner piling. He could hear nothing overhead, but out on the lake he saw a wide platform floating on the surface. An anchor chain extended from one corner into the water.

Neither Takana nor Montague could be seen.

But once his eyes adjusted to the sun's glare off the water he saw Molly out there, lying unmoving on her back, rocking side to side as the water around her began to boil.

Damn, he thought, and moved quickly to the front, scanning the shore for signs of a boat, then ducking back into the cabin's shadow when he heard footsteps on the porch.

"You get on with it," said Takana.

"Well, hurry," Montague answered. "I don't want him to miss this."

"He won't."

"He will if you don't fetch him."

"You don't speak to me like that, Partridge."

"I'll speak to you any way I want to, you squinty-eyed little beetle. Now get him or he's going to miss the show. And this time it won't be my fault."

The corner ladder quivered, and Takana climbed down, had reached the second rung above the ground when Lincoln darted out his hand, grabbed his ankle and toppled him off. Takana yelled as he fell, and yelled no more when Lincoln put an apologetic but firm heel into his throat. Then he scrambled up as fast as he could and saw Montague standing in front of the doorway, the Soldier in his hand, the patch up and pointing toward the lake.

There were no laser-beam lights, no vision-blinding bolts of lightning; there was only the Soldier of a dead god with sword raised and both eyes open.

In a way, he would have preferred the lasers.

Montague heard him but didn't turn. "You're too late, Mr. Blackthorne," he said as Linc approached cautiously. "You might as well get comfortable and watch."

"For god's sake," he said, "that's your sister out there!"

"Yes, I know that."

"Well?"

"Well what? She's crazy as a loon."

"And you're not, for working with Cull?"

"She wanted to stop my research."

"Cull killed your father."

"He was crazy too."

Linc grabbed the single railing for support, wondering what in hell he had to say to this man to prevent him from murdering his own flesh and blood. He looked out to the lake, and the platform was rocking more precipitously now, the water bubbling, smoking, and sending waves across its surface that rocked even the seaplane on its pontoons.

His hold on the railing tightened—Molly was waking up, her arms flailing vainly for some sort of hold on the smooth, unbroken wood.

Lincoln braced himself to jump.

"Don't," Montague warned, finally turning his head. "I've never tried using this on a human being, but I will if you try to stop me."

Molly shrieked.

Montague looked back and waved.

Lincoln lunged forward, head down and arms wide, and engulfed the taller man in his grip. Partridge slammed an elbow down on his back, but momentum shoved him off-balance and he was forced to thumb down the patch and deal with the intruder. But by that time they were already at the far side of the porch, Partridge striking the railing first.

The thin wood splintered.

Lincoln thought he was flying.

The ground reached them, and he used the bearded man to absorb most of the landing, making sure he wouldn't move again by keeping his head pressed against Montague's stomach. Then he rolled to one side and stared at the sky. His arms were killing him, his legs felt as if they'd be delighted with amputation, and his own lungs were struggling to find a way to work.

Montague didn't move.

The Soldier lay between them.

I will not move, he decided; I will stay here and make pictures from the clouds and drink the rain and let the native girls bring me ambrosia and coconut milk. I'll grow a beard. I'll live off the land. I'll learn to make thread from vines and suits from ferns.

"Oh Jesus," he groaned, and sat up, holding his head.

Molly called to him frantically, and he rubbed his eyes to clear them, saw that the lake had subsided and she was standing, semaphoring with her hands that he should stop lying around and get her on dry land, instantly if not sooner.

He smiled and waved back, pushed himself to his feet and leaned against the nearest piling until his head stopped spinning and his stomach stopped producing acid that made him gag.

She screamed again.

He waved again.

She screamed so high-pitched he wanted to cover his ears, and he turned away for a moment, and saw the shadow on the ground—the shadow of a man standing above him with a bow and arrow in his hands.

He looked up.

Florenz Cull smiled down.

"Would you shoot an unarmed man?" Lincoln asked him.

Cull would.

TWENTY-FOUR

LINC THREW HIMSELF UNDER THE CABIN, LOSING HIS balance in the process and landing on his rump. The arrow dug into the ground several feet to one side of where he had been standing, and he supposed that the man had closed his eye to aim. A mistake when the closed eye wasn't the one with the patch.

On his feet again he heard Cull stomping along the porch, and he followed beneath him, waiting for an opportunity to do something constructive for a change. They made a complete circle of the cabin feinting sprints and escapes before Cull stopped.

The Soldier lay in the sunlight.

"Mr. Blackthorne?"

"Right here," he said.

"A sporting proposition."

"I'm listening."

"If you can reach our little friend before I put an arrow through your back, you may have it and leave my island in peace."

"And if I don't?"

"You won't be around for my coronation."

What, he thought, were the chances of Cull closing his good eye again? What, he thought further, where the chances of hell freezing over in the tropics?

"I don't think so, Florrie."

"Then we have a stalemate."

"Oh, I don't know about that."

Cull laughed.

Lincoln looked out to the float and saw Molly on her knees, one fist pounding her leg while the other hand pulled at her hair. She had every right to be upset, he knew, but hysterics weren't going to get her anywhere.

He looked up and saw Cull's shadow in the tiny gaps between the porch's floorboards. It was clever the way these places had been built, admirable the way they hadn't used any nails but rather the local flora to bind the logs and slats together, to seal them in such a way that not even a mosquito could squeeze through. Of course, he thought as he slipped his knife from its sheath and put it between his teeth, wrapped his hands around an inner piling and began to shimmy up, all that traffic is bound to loosen a few things here and there, and accidents will happen even to the best of us.

It had occurred to him to attempt to poke the blade through the breaks in the flooring, but they were ten feet over his head; he would have to jump with one arm extended, and with his luck he'd probably stick the knife into the wood and be unable to free it.

"Mr. Blackthorne?"

As close to the top as he dared to get, he took the

knife from his mouth and began to saw at the thick vines.

"I hear you."

"I have another proposition."

He grunted loudly.

"I will toss down the keys to the seaplane. You will go there, coast over to Miss Partridge, who is going to be bald rather soon, I think, and take her with you off the island."

"And . . . you . . . get . . . the Soldier?"

"Of course."

The vine parted; Lincoln dropped and held his breath.

The plank didn't fall.

Hell, he thought, and scowled at the splinters he plucked from his arms.

"Y'know, Whitey," he said, "this is dumb."

"Do not *call* me that!" Cull yelled. "That is a disparagement upon my mother, and I've already told you I will not have it! Do you hear me, tailor? I will not have it!"

Cull stamped his foot angrily.

The plank parted.

Cull yelled and dropped through, and Lincoln was positioned to lunge at him and bring him down when he saw that the man had landed on his feet.

Damn, he thought; being seven feet tall has its advantages.

"Well," Cull said with a wolfish grin, reached out suddenly and snared Linc's arm. Linc aimed a side kick at his groin, and Cull sidestepped, spinning him closer to land a punch on his cheek. Linc grunted, snapped his head back and managed a blow into the man's midsection. The man lost a bit of air, but didn't release him. He would have tried another kick then, but Cull grabbed the front of his shirt and lifted him off the ground. Linc encircled his neck and pulled his head near, then leaned to one side and screamed in Cull's ear.

Cull laughed.

Nuts, Linc thought; he's shut the aids off.

Then Cull stiffened his arms and Linc flailed his fists wildly, grimacing as his blows landed weakly on Cull's shoulders while Cull walked forward slowly between the pilings toward the lake.

Molly screamed.

Cull shifted one hand to Linc's throat and began to squeeze.

Linc saw the man's arms bend slightly under the strain and he reached out to bury his hands in the mass of white hair. He pulled as hard as he could.

Cull shrieked.

Linc pulled harder and saw droplets of blood begin to seep through the white; again, and his right hand came away with a fistful of hair he shoved in Cull's face. At the same time, he snapped his other hand down onto the crook of the man's elbow, and Cull released him with a groan. Linc landed on his feet and wasted no time butting his chest to drive him back; Cull caught an arm and swung him into a piling. There was red, and sparkling light, and he was swung out again, back again, but this time he cushioned most of the blow with a backward-extended foot that he used to launch himself forward. Cull's arm gave at the pressure, and Linc took hold of his hair again, wrapped his legs around the man's waist, and pulled.

Cull shrieked and put a forearm under his chin.

Lincoln twisted away and bit his nose.

Cull yelled, covered the nose, and Linc wriggled free, blinked the sweat from his eyes, and kicked him in the groin. Cull doubled over. Linc grabbed two fistfuls of what hair was left and spun the man around, releasing him with a toe into his ribs when they were parallel to the water.

Cull stumbled in, fell, rose sputtering in a sitting position, and windmilled his arms as he tried to regain his footing.

Linc sprinted for the Soldier, held it tightly, and after taking a deep breath, lifted the patch.

The water around Cull began to boil, and the man began to scream. His face reddened, and the blood on his scalp began to pour more freely over his face. He lurched to his feet and tried to run, but the smoke lifting from the surface blinded him and he ran in the wrong direction—out toward the center instead of toward shore, until he screamed one more time and vanished.

The lake bubbled.

The bubbles were red.

Linc thumbed the patch down and dropped the Soldier at his feet, his hands trembling too much to hold it.

Molly screamed.

Lincoln had had enough. He stalked to the water's edge and put his hands on his hips.

"Goddamnit," he said, "it's over so shut the hell up!"

She quieted suddenly, looked at him, then screamed again. "You idiot! Look at the damned water!"

It was still boiling, more furiously than ever.

It took a while for the implications to sink in; then he gestured for her to remain calm, ran back to the far cabin just as Lymington was staggering into the sunlight. Linc shouted at him to hurry, explained the situation as the old pilot stumbled down the ladder, and practically dragged him out to the dock and into the waiting, bobbing seaplane.

"Damnit, I don't have the keys!" he said, slapping the instrument panel.

"Don't need them," Lymington assured him.

"What are you going to do, Ace, hot-wire it?"

Lymington sniffed, pulled a set of keys out of his pocket, and soon had the engine revving. Lincoln cast off the rope holding them to the dock and they bounced and bucked their way to the float and took Molly aboard.

She glared at him and strapped herself in.

He glared at her and did the same.

Lymington hummed to himself and within minutes had them in the air. "I believe," he said over his shoulder, "we had best head back for the islands."

"Fine," Lincoln said, looking out the window to his right as they banked sharply. Then he groaned.

"What?" Molly snapped.

"I forgot the Soldier."

"You called me an idiot!"

"But I don't think we'll have to worry. Angel, you'd better not hang around."

Lymington nodded.

"Hey, Lincoln, you called me an idiot!"

He turned to her, measured the distance between her chin and his fist, and praised his self-control when, instead of punching her, he pointed. She resisted for a full five seconds before looking out and seeing the vast cloud of steam and smoke rising from the center of Kampollea.

"It's going to blow up," she said in quiet astonishment.

"Looks that way."

"My brother—"

"He was already dead, Molly. I'm sorry."

She shuddered and lowered her head. "That's all right. He was crazy anyway." A sigh, and she looked out again, one hand touching the pane and tracing its outline. "Nice, but crazy."

"The Soldier, too. I'm sorry we had to leave it. It would have made you a very wealthy woman."

"That's okay," she told him. "I'm rich anyway. Another couple of million more or less won't make any difference."

"You're rich?"

"Sure. How do you think I paid for all those airline tickets? My good looks? Wow, look at that thing go!"

"You're rich?"

"God, Angel, we'd better be almost there before it blows or it'll knock us right out of the air."

He sat back and stared at her profile. Then the plane dropped in a downdraft and he closed his eyes tightly, whispering silently to his stomach not to get so excited. It wouldn't be long before they were back in Honolulu. Then he was going to get on the first boat back to the mainland, the first train back to the East Coast, and rent a limousine to bring him back to his tailor shop in Inverness, New Jersey. He was going to sleep for a week or two, then look up a few friends and let them know what he thought of them.

After that, he was going to go to the Bronx Zoo and spend the whole day looking at a moose.

They landed without incident on Oahu, only barely resisting dropping to their knees to kiss the ground. Then, not brooking any delays, Lincoln snared a cab to the docks. Molly went with him after promising to join Lymington later.

"Lincoln?"

"What?"

"We . . . that is, we won't be seeing each other again, will we? After we land, I mean."

"I guess not."

"Will . . . I mean, I don't mean to be forward, but what I mean is, even though I haven't said it yet, but will you be glad? Not to see me again, I mean."

It was a close call between tact and truth.

"Not really," he compromised.

"Funny," she said, so thoughtfully he opened his eyes to look at her. "I don't think I'll be sorry at all. I don't mean to criticize, you understand, but you're really no fun. No fun at all."

He closed his eyes again, felt the bruises on his ribs, the scrapes on his arms, the scratches and aches in his legs, and sighed. Crazy as a loon, he thought, and did not open his eyes again until they arrived. The ticket was purchased, the ship was already boarding, and they walked quickly toward the dock.

"Maybe," she said softly, "I'll call you when you get back."

He smiled gently. "Okay. I'd like that."

A purser rushed by, bleating the same message they could hear over the loudspeakers—all visitors ashore, the ship was departing. He kissed her once, quickly, and hurried up the gangplank, found a place on the railing and saw her below. He waved as horns blew and confetti filled the air and a band below played "Aloha." She waved back. He blew her a kiss. She started to wave with both arms as the ship pulled away. He laughed and blew her another kiss. She waved even harder, and he couldn't figure out why she was so delirious until a soft hand touched his shoulder.

"Lincoln," Salome said, "you owe me several thousand dollars, you son of a bitch."

Then he heard Arturo singing.

He was not reminded of angels.

ABOUT THE AUTHOR

After studying at Trinity College, Cambridge, Geoffrey Marsh immigrated to the United States and taught literature at the Sloan Campion School. He is the author of two previous Lincoln Blackthorne adventures, *The King of Satan's Eyes* and *The Tail of the Arabian, Knight.* He lives in New Jersey.